———— ★ ————

"Ford?" Rhodes said, walking slowly toward the open door.

There was a king-size bed in the room. It had red satin sheets. There was a mirror on the ceiling that Rhodes strongly suspected hadn't been installed by the original owners, who had been staunch Presbyterians.

The current owner, Hayes Ford, was staring wide-eyed at his reflection in the mirror as he lay on his back on the right side of the bed. He was wearing a red robe that gapped open over white satin boxer shorts with red hearts on them. The hearts matched the sheets, but Ford didn't care. He didn't care about anything. He was dead.

If Ford had been alive to take the wager, Rhodes would have bet him that the bullet came from the same pistol that had killed Brady Meredith.

———— ★ ————

"The humor, the suspense, and the small-town ambience all ring true."

—Booklist

Previously published Worldwide Mystery titles by
BILL CRIDER

DEATH BY ACCIDENT
...A DANGEROUS THING

WINNING CAN BE MURDER

BILL CRIDER

WORLDWIDE®

TORONTO • NEW YORK • LONDON
AMSTERDAM • PARIS • SYDNEY • HAMBURG
STOCKHOLM • ATHENS • TOKYO • MILAN
MADRID • WARSAW • BUDAPEST • AUCKLAND

Another one for Judy

WINNING CAN BE MURDER

A Worldwide Mystery/July 2000

First published by St. Martin's Press, Incorporated.

ISBN 0-373-26354-6

Printed in U.S.A.

WINNING
CAN BE
MURDER

ONE

ON CERTAIN LATE-FALL evenings in most small Texas towns, Sheriff Dan Rhodes thought, you could actually *smell* football in the air. It smelled like the first cool days of the season and burning leaves and popcorn and roasted peanuts and leather.

You could hear it, too. You could hear the bands tuning up in the grandstand and then playing "Them Basses" and "March Grandioso" and the school fight song. You could hear the play-by-play announcer's echoing voice reminding everyone to make a trip to the concession stand sponsored by the Band Boosters Club for a refreshing soft drink before the game.

And of course you could see it. You could see the dust motes drifting through the headlights of the last cars arriving at the field, and you could see the haze of yellow light that hung over the field itself, often the only place in town where any lights were on, because everyone was at the game.

Some people said that high school football was almost as important as religion to people in Texas, but Rhodes knew better. It was *more* important. People just didn't want to admit it.

Rhodes, however, didn't think that Billy Graham at the height of his powers—or even a tag-team duo of Graham and Billy Sunday—could have filled the high school stadiums in every city and town in Texas for ten weeks every fall; not for fifty or sixty years in a row. But high school football could. And did. It didn't matter whether the home team had a winning record. The crowds came out just the same.

On this particular fall evening, practically everyone in Clearview, and for that matter in most of Blacklin County, with the exception of the sheriff, was riding the wave of the kind of elation that comes to small towns only occasionally in their history—when the high school team is headed for the state play-offs.

Winning a state championship meant something to a town. You could tell when you saw the signs erected at the city limits of every community whose team had won one. Some of the school colors on the signs were faded by time, the metal flecked with rust, but the signs themselves were still there:

WELCOME TO MEXIA
HOME OF THE *MEXIA BLACKCATS!*
TEXAS HIGH SCHOOL STATE 3-A FOOTBALL
CHAMPIONS
1988!

A state championship was something which, up until this year, people in Clearview had only dreamed of. The Clearview High team had never won one. A team had come close once, in 1949, and people still talked about it at Lee's drugstore on Saturday mornings, where the town's biggest fans met the coaches for coffee and hashed over the previous evening's game. They remembered the players' names, their numbers, and all the ways in which the big game had gone wrong for Clearview.

The game had been played somewhere in the Texas Panhandle, and while Rhodes had once known quite well the name of the winning school, he could no longer recall it. He had been too young to go to the game, but his father had gone and had talked about what happened for weeks afterward. Clearview had lost fifty-four to seven.

"When those Panhandle boys ran out on the field," he'd said, "I thought they were going to kill our boys."

"You don't mean that," Rhodes's mother said. "You shouldn't exaggerate so much."

She had been standing at the stove, Rhodes recalled, wearing a white apron with blue stitching as she fried chicken in a heavy iron skillet.

"I do mean it," his father said. "I really thought they were going to kill our boys."

Rhodes's father always came into the kitchen to talk to his wife while supper was being prepared. Sometimes they listened to "One Man's Family" on the radio, but mostly they talked.

"They were so big," he went on, "they made our boys look like peewee leaguers. I swear there were two or three of 'em that looked like they were thirty years old. Every one of them probably has to shave twice a day with an Eversharp Schick."

Rhodes's mother turned over a piece of chicken in the skillet with a long two-pronged fork. Grease popped and hissed.

"It'll be a long time before we get that far in the play-offs again," Rhodes's father said, shaking his head. "A long, long time."

It had been longer than anyone had really thought, more than forty years, but it looked as if the time had come at last: the time for Clearview to erase the memory of a humiliation that had lasted for generations.

Which explained why everyone in town, everyone in the whole county, was elated.

Except Rhodes. To the sheriff, the fact that the Clearview Catamounts had won every district game except the last, the one that was being played this evening, meant something quite different—especially on a Friday night.

It meant minors consuming alcoholic beverages; it meant too many arrests for DWI; it meant gambling, often enough right out in the open, in the parking lot near the stadium; it meant fights at every club in town; it meant making sure that the rivalries on the field didn't spill across the sidelines, onto the benches and into the stands; and it meant pulling his deputies in from patrol on Friday nights so they could police the area.

It also meant a considerable bit of worry about something that, so far as Rhodes knew, had never happened anywhere in Texas. If anyone wanted to burglarize on a large scale, a Friday night like this one would be the perfect time. There probably were more deserted homes in most small towns than there were occupied ones.

In fact, Rhodes wondered why whole towns hadn't

been looted before now. Even the stores and banks were practically begging to be robbed. Maybe it hadn't happened, he thought, because all the crooks were football fans, too. They were probably at the games.

Even if they were, Rhodes still didn't like the possibilities, though he had to admit to himself as he walked toward the stadium that he did like the games. And this one promised to be a good one.

The Catamounts had won all their district games to this point by an average of something like twenty points. Their opponents tonight, the Garton Greyhounds, who were favored to win by a touchdown, were also undefeated in the district. They had outscored their opposition by an even wider margin than the Catamounts, thanks to a running back who had averaged nearly two hundred yards a game and had college recruiters from California to Florida and all points north drooling on their scouting reports.

Now the last car was parked and Rhodes could hear the cheers of the crowd building in intensity. Any second now, the Garton band would play its school song, which would be followed by the Clearview song and finally "The Star-Spangled Banner." It was time for Rhodes to make a last circuit of the stands and then to meet Ivy at the main gate. If he hurried, he might make it in time for the kickoff.

RHODES WAS DELAYED on his way to the grandstand, however, by the sight of two men standing near the fence that surrounded the stadium. They were at the far north end, and with the lights directed at the field and away from the parking lot, they were almost hidden in the gathering darkness.

Rhodes recognized one of them anyway: Hayes Ford, a short, sharp-featured, mousy man who was Clearview's leading gambler—not that anything had ever been proved against him.

Everyone knew that Ford took bets on the Friday night games, but no one had ever been able to catch him at it. One year Rhodes had even brought in an undercover officer from a neighboring county, who had attempted to place a bet with Ford. But the rodentlike gambler had seemed somehow to sense the presence of law and had refused to take the proffered money. In fact, he had pretended to have no idea of what the officer was suggesting, as if he were shocked—shocked!—to hear that someone might actually be placing wagers on a sporting contest.

Rhodes thought about that episode as he started toward the men, who were now in close conversation. If a bet was being discussed right now, maybe there would be money exchanged. And if there was, maybe Rhodes would see it.

Rhodes should have known better. He hadn't gone more than a few steps before Ford looked up and glanced in the sheriff's direction. As soon as he saw who was coming, he said something to the other man, who immediately walked away along the high fence that surrounded the field, and after some distance turned toward the end zone, though Rhodes didn't think he would be admitted to the field through that entrance.

The man was considerably taller than Ford, probably well over six feet, but that was all Rhodes could tell about him. He couldn't see the man's face.

Rhodes didn't figure there was any use in going after him. He would probably go on around to the other side of the field and enter the stands there, mingling with the crowd before the sheriff could get to him. So Rhodes kept on walking toward Ford, who stood waiting patiently, his hands in the pockets of a dark-colored windbreaker.

When Rhodes got a little closer, he could see that the jacket was blue and trimmed in gold, and he knew that on the back would be a gold bobcat head surrounded by gold letters spelling out CLEARVIEW CATAMOUNTS. One thing you had to give Ford credit for, he had school spirit.

"Who's your money on?" Rhodes asked just as the Garton band struck up the school song. On the parking lot, the notes were muffled by the grandstand.

"I don't know what you mean, Sheriff," Ford said, ducking his head and brushing at his pointy little nose. "That's a kind of insulting question to ask a fella. I don't put my money on anybody. I'm just a fan like you."

"Sure you are," Rhodes said. "Who was that you were just talking to?"

Ford looked around. "Talking to? There's nobody around here to talk to."

"You know what I mean, Ford."

Ford ducked his head again. "Oh, you must be talking about that fella that was here before you walked up. Just a friend, Sheriff. Nobody you'd know."

Rhodes didn't push it. He knew it wouldn't do any good. "Why don't we go in to the game?" he asked.

Ford was about to answer, but there was a huge cheer from the stands as the Greyhound band finished playing.

"We better just stand here," Ford said as the cheering died down and the strains of the Clearview alma mater drifted into the night air. "Wouldn't be respectful to walk while the school song's being played."

Rhodes didn't see it that way. He left Ford, who was singing the Clearview school song in a ragged baritone, and started toward the main gate.

IVY WASN'T AT THE GATE when Rhodes got there. She had gone on into the stadium. Rhodes got to his seat just in time for "The Star Spangled Banner," to which he sang along, though he had never been able to hit the high notes.

"I thought you weren't going to make it," Ivy said as cheers erupted around them.

They sat down on the hard wooden bench. Most of the people around them were still standing, yelling loudly and waving Catamount pennants. The cheerleaders were on the other side of the field, bouncing around in front of the student section of the bleachers, but that didn't affect the crowd's enthusiasm.

"I wouldn't miss the kickoff," Rhodes said.

The teams ran on the field and the Greyhound kicker set down the tee.

Rhodes gave a satisfied nod. "We're receiving."

Ivy smiled at him. "Are you thinking about 'Will-o'-the-Wisp Dan Rhodes' again?"

"I never think about that guy," Rhodes told her. But that wasn't true. He did.

Probably everyone who had ever played football had memories of at least one special game, and the one Rhodes recalled was the first of his junior year, in fact his very first varsity game. It was also his last varsity game, his last game of any kind, but that was beside the point.

The point was that in those days, Rhodes had been slim and fast, neither of which he was now, and he had been the Clearview Catamounts' kick return man.

He remembered every single thing about the opening kickoff of that first game: the way the ball sounded when the kicker's foot struck it, the way the ball turned over in the lights as it arced toward him, and the way the ball stung his hands and nearly knocked him down when he caught it. People who've never taken in a kickoff have no idea how hard the ball hits when it comes down.

In spite of the force with which the ball struck him, Rhodes caught it cleanly and started straight up the field. From the stands the field might look cluttered up with players, but down on the grass it wasn't like that at all. Twenty-two teenagers didn't take up a lot of room, and a football field is more than a hundred yards long and over fifty yards wide; five-thousand-plus square yards when you figure it up. There can be a lot of gaps between teenagers, and

Rhodes found every one of them. He zigged and he zagged, he hip-faked and dodged, and suddenly he was in the open, running for his life.

No one caught him until the instant he crossed the goal line, when two players crashed into him from behind. He'd been fast, but there were others who were faster. They hadn't kept him from scoring, though.

Rhodes was so elated by the touchdown that he didn't even feel his leg break. He hadn't even known it was broken until he tried to stand up and found that he couldn't do it. The trainer and the assistant coach had finally strapped him to a stretcher and carried him off the field.

The story in the newspaper the next day referred to him as "Will-o'-the-Wisp Dan Rhodes" and called him the hero of the game, which the newspaper called a "defensive struggle." Clearview had won by a score of only six to nothing because, in the excitement of the kick return followed by the injury, the Clearview kicker had missed the extra point.

Rhodes's broken leg kept him out of the rest of the games that year, which was just as well, since the six-to-nothing win was also the last Clearview victory for a long time. In fact, the team lost several games by more than fifty points. Rhodes liked to think that the team would have won more had he been playing, but he knew he was only kidding himself. Even a will-'o-the-wisp couldn't make that much difference.

The next year, though Rhodes's leg had healed completely, he had lost most of his speed. He tried out for the team again, but the coach told him that there really wasn't any place for him. He was too small to play in the line and too slow to play in the backfield, either offense or defense.

So he had gotten a job after school and determined not to worry about football, but of course he'd never forgotten about his being Will-o'-the-Wisp, though just about everyone else had. Ivy liked to twit him about it now and then, but no one else ever mentioned it, which Rhodes supposed was just as well.

He wouldn't want to be like some of the men he could see from where he sat, Jerry Tabor for one. Tabor still wore his fraying, thirty-year-old Clearview letter jacket and stood as near the sidelines as he could, as if hoping that someone would remember when he was one of the best running backs in the district—instead of a not very successful used-car salesman for Del-Ray Chevrolet. These days, Tabor seemed to feel that he somehow shared in the team's glory, and maybe he did. The team's success reminded people vaguely of Tabor's glory days, and he'd been interviewed by the newspaper and invited to speak at several pep rallies.

The Clearview kick receiver this year wasn't as fast or as tricky as Rhodes had been. He got only about ten yards before being swarmed by Garton Greyhounds.

"Want some popcorn?" Rhodes asked Ivy.

"Only if there's no butter on it," she said.

Rhodes sighed, but he went to get the popcorn.

TWO

THE GAME WASN'T as satisfying as Rhodes had hoped. Both teams were so intense that a fight broke out practically every time there was a hard tackle. Nothing serious, nothing that required the ejection of a player, but tempers were high and Rhodes was afraid that it wouldn't take much to set off a real melee.

He was right. Late in the third quarter, with the score tied at twenty-one, the Garton punt returner broke free from the pack at the thirty and sprinted down the far sideline. A Catamount player had an angle on him, however, and caught up with him at about the fifty. He barreled into him, sending him flying into the Greyhound bench.

Rhodes wasn't sure, but it looked to him as if the runner might have stepped out of bounds just before getting hit.

Unlike Rhodes, the Garton bench *was* sure. The Catamount tackler disappeared under a pile of red-and-white jerseys.

The Catamount bench cleared in an instant as players charged to help out their teammate. The entire Catamount squad, including the trainers, tore across the field toward the heaving pile of Greyhounds. The coaches were right behind the team.

Rhodes hoped they were trying to calm things down, but it was hard to tell.

The Greyhound coaches were trying to drag players off the pile, or so it seemed. Later, Rhodes wondered if they might not have been encouraging them.

Jerry Tabor, his frayed letter jacket flapping, clambered over the fence that separated the field from the stands and started after the coaches. Rhodes could see his mouth working, but he could not hear what he was yelling because of the crowd noise.

"Uh-oh," Ivy said, but Rhodes was already on his way onto the field.

CROSSING THE FIELD, Rhodes was surprised at how little certain things had changed in all the years since he'd played football. The browning grass crunched under his feet, the sound of the crowd was still a dull roar, and the noise that really stood out was the thudding of pads and helmets. It was too bad that the thudding was taking place in a fight instead of in the course of a game.

Ruth Grady, one of Rhodes's deputies, was already in the middle of things when Rhodes arrived. She was short and stocky and well able to take care of herself in most situations. She had shouldered her way into the middle of the fighting that was breaking out along the sidelines and was trying to get to the pile that still writhed in front of the Greyhound bench.

The situation bordered on bedlam. Players were screaming things about each other's lineage and mental capacities as they tried to punch each other out. It wasn't easy to punch out someone wearing a football helmet, but there was some damage being done to players who hadn't had the presence of mind to put their headgear on. Most of the damage was inflicted by players who also had their helmets off but who were swinging them at other unprotected heads.

The officials were trying vainly to separate the brawling players, but they were having no success at all. In fact, one of them was sitting on the grass with a dazed look on his face as if he might have been clobbered by a helmet.

The Clearview coaches had managed to grab a few of their players and muscle them away from the main part of the fighting, but the players were still struggling, trying to get back to the fray.

Jerry Tabor was having words with a woman who had come out of the Garton crowd and run onto the field. She would be easy to pick out of a lineup, if it came to that: the hair on one side of her head was dyed a garish red, while the other side was pure white, the Garton colors. Her face was also painted in contrasting shades, white on the side under the red hair and red under the white hair.

Jerry was trying to get her off the field, but he wasn't having much luck. She kept kicking him in the shins. Rhodes didn't know whom to rescue first, the downed Catamount player or Tabor.

Suddenly he heard the opening notes of "The Star Spangled Banner." The Clearview Marching Catamounts to the rescue, he thought, as the cheerleaders bravely tried to get the crowd to sing along. But the national anthem didn't do a bit of good. The fight continued as if the band were not playing at all. Rhodes suspected that the only person in the stadium who was standing at attention was Hayes Ford.

Rhodes started throwing players aside, trying to get to the center of things. He could see Ruth Grady grabbing at shoulder pads as she tried without much success to unpile the irate Greyhounds still atop the hapless Catamount tackler.

Then Rhodes heard another sound that cut through all the grunts and groans and screaming and even the blare of the national anthem.

Rhodes looked around. The ambulance that usually parked in the south end zone in case of emergency was headed across the field. The piercing siren got everyone's attention, and the fact that the ambulance was bearing down on them at about twenty miles an hour did more to stop the fighting than anything else could have. Players, officials, and coaches scattered for the fence, jamming together in the gate. Some of the more agile ones, like Jerry Tabor, who had abandoned the painted woman, went right over the fence.

Even the pileup near the Garton bench broke apart, with players rolling wildly right and left to escape the oncoming ambulance. The driver threw on the brakes, but the tires skidded in the grass and the vehicle narrowly missed Rhodes, who hadn't moved, before it careened into the Greyhound benches and sent one of them flying onto the track.

The ambulance came to a stop then and Lawton, the Blacklin County jailer, got out. He looked to

Rhodes, a little bit like Lou Costello, though he was at least seventy years old.

"Damn driver was at the concession stand, I guess," Lawton said. "I had to drive this thing myself. Like not to've got it stopped."

"So I noticed," Rhodes said. "Thank goodness you didn't kill anybody."

Lawton was outraged. "Kill anybody? What're you talkin' about? Of course I didn't kill anybody. What I did was save a bunch of lives, and you oughta consider yourself lucky that I was here at the game. What'd you have done if I hadn't turned on that siren? Got your head knocked off, is what. But don't thank me. After all, I'm just a worthless old man who's tryin' to do the best for ever'body. I'm just—"

Rhodes held up a hand to stop him. "Thanks, Lawton. I didn't mean to criticize. You did just fine."

"You don't really mean that. You're just tryin' to calm me down so I don't have a heart attack. Wouldn't want that on your conscience, would you? The worthless old man who saves your life has a heart attack and dies right on the spot. That wouldn't look good in the papers, now would it?"

Lawton usually got into that kind of dispute with Hack Jensen, the dispatcher, but since Hack wasn't around, Rhodes was an acceptable substitute. The sheriff didn't mind. Lawton had a point, in a way.

"I said you did fine, and I meant it. Now let's see if we can get this mob straightened out and start the game again."

Lawton shook his head. "'Bout time you thought of that. Wonder how many of these boys the refs'll kick out?"

Rhodes didn't have an answer for that one. The referees did, but only after a consultation that must have lasted at least fifteen minutes.

They walked practically to the goalpost and huddled together with Rhodes and Ruth Grady standing guard to keep players and coaches at bay. Lawton tagged along, too. Rhodes didn't try to stop him.

What the referees eventually decided was to eject two of the Garton Greyhounds who in their judgment were the first two to leave the bench and attack the Clearview tackler. The Catamounts were not penalized, the officials having concluded that the runner was in bounds when he was hit.

As soon as he heard the decision, the Garton head coach turned purple and hopped up and down like a kid on a pogo stick as an official tried to calm him down.

"What do you think his blood pressure is right now?" Ruth Grady asked.

"I'd guess about two hunnerd over a hunnered and fifty," Lawton said. "I expect there's a stethoscope in that ambulance if you want to check it."

The ambulance driver had come out onto the field and retrieved his vehicle, returning it to its usual spot behind the goalposts. He hadn't said a word to Lawton about commandeering it.

"I'm not much of a nurse," Ruth said. "What about you, Sheriff?"

Rhodes wasn't much of a nurse, either, but he

thought that the Garton coach might be an interesting study for some medical student. He hadn't cooled off a bit, and he continued to scream at the referee and bounce around the field.

Rhodes walked over, and between the two of them, he and the ref got the coach back to the bench, where his players and assistants had confined themselves to muttering vague threats, spiced up by the occasional vulgar gesture.

"Just lettin' the crowd know they think they're Number One," Lawton explained to Ruth, who managed to keep a straight face.

Somehow order was finally restored, and the game picked up more or less where it had left off. Garton had the ball on their own forty-eight yard line; the Greyhounds—possibly inspired by the fighting, the ejection of their return man, and the fact that the Catamounts got no penalty—promptly ripped off three first downs in a row. Then, on the next play, they scored. And they kicked the point.

Score: Garton 28, Clearview 21.

It stayed that way until the last minute of the game. The Clearview fans grew gloomier and gloomier as the Greyhound supporters became more and more cheerful, and more and more vocal about their team's prowess. The woman with the red and white hair even joined the Garton cheerleaders for a yell, which made the fans still more gleeful.

None of the Clearview followers left the stands, but it was obvious that many of them had given up hope. Things looked especially bleak after the Greyhounds punted the ball all the way to the Catamount five-yard line. A draw play gained ten yards and a first down, but then two passes were incomplete and it was fourth down.

Ivy touched Rhodes's arm. "It's all over, isn't it?"

Rhodes shook his head. "There are thirty seconds left. Remember what Yogi Berra said. 'It ain't over till it's over.'"

Rhodes didn't really believe that, however; nor did anyone else in the crowd. But then the Catamount quarterback took the snap, scrambled around for several seconds, and heaved a desperation pass from his own ten-yard line. A skinny receiver flew past the defender, ran under the ball at the fifty-yard line, and kept right on going, reaching the end zone untouched.

The Clearview bench erupted in a fit of ecstasy unmatched in Catamount history, with the fans screaming themselves hoarse, while the Greyhounds' supporters sat as stunned as if someone had hit them in the head with a wooden mallet. There was so much screaming and yelling for Clearview that Rhodes couldn't even hear the band playing the fight song, though he could see the director's arms waving.

Rhodes wasn't as happy as everyone else seemed to be. He could foresee a big problem for the Clearview team. If the game ended in a tie, Clearview would lose.

Tie games were decided on the basis of two statistics: penetrations—the number of times one team had been inside the other's twenty-yard-line—and first downs. Penetrations came first, and by Rhodes's count Garton led on penetrations by a six-to-five margin.

The Catamounts had to go for two points.

The joy on the bench died down quickly as the Clearview head coach, Jasper Knowles, held a heated discussion with his offensive coach, Brady Meredith.

Knowles was about fifty-five, a short, bald man with a head like a bowling ball and a body to match. If he fell down, you could probably roll him across the field. Meredith, a former college quarterback about twenty years younger than Knowles, towered over the older man, but Knowles wasn't backing away.

"What's happening?" Ivy asked.

"Looks like Jasper doesn't like the play Brady called," Rhodes said.

The crowd roared as the coaches yelled at each other. Rhodes tried to make out the coaches' words, but it was impossible.

Then Meredith threw a punch at Knowles, who ducked to the side. The punch grazed his ear, and he stepped back, staring at Meredith in surprise. The younger coach took the opportunity to spit at Knowles's feet and walk away.

The stadium fell suddenly quiet, as if everyone there had taken a simultaneous deep breath.

Knowles took his own deep breath, and stood up as straight as he could. Without looking at Meredith, he put his arms around the quarterback's shoulders and whispered something to him. The quarterback ran onto the field, but not without a look backward, as if he were seeking some kind of confirmation from Meredith.

If that was what he was looking for, he didn't find it. Meredith was already leaving the field, followed closely by Jerry Tabor, who'd had an excellent view of the entire proceedings from his place by the fence.

All this activity had been closely observed by the Garton coach, but he didn't have to call anything to the attention of the referees. They penalized Clearview five yards for delay of game.

"That makes it harder, doesn't it?" Ivy said.

Rhodes nodded. He hoped that Knowles had called a good play. If he hadn't, the fans, already stirred to a state of hysteria by the earlier fight and the excitement of the last-minute touchdown, were likely to storm the field and lynch him.

The Catamount quarterback called out the signals, took the ball from center, faked a handoff, and dropped back to pass. Somehow a Garton linebacker slipped a blocker and leapt toward the quarterback, his hands upraised.

The quarterback threw the ball straight up, or so it seemed from where Rhodes was sitting. It must have had a slight angle on it, because it got by the linebacker's hands and came down in the end zone, right among a cluster of six or seven players, Catamounts and Greyhounds, all of whom jumped into the air with outstretched arms.

The ball landed somewhere among them, and they fell in a heap as the officials converged on them.

Before they got there, a player in blue and gold squirmed out of the stack, the ball clutched in his arms. He ran about five yards before he raised the ball over his head and did a little dance that he must have invented himself.

Ivy stood on tiptoe and put her mouth to Rhodes's ear to tell him something, but the crowd had gone berserk. He couldn't hear a word she was saying.

THREE

IT'S AN UNFORTUNATE part of the rules of football that a game must be played to its conclusion.

After scoring a touchdown, even if only a few seemingly meaningless seconds are left in the game, the team that scored has to kick off to the other team because of the possibility that those final seconds could take on a completely unexpected meaning.

For one thing, as small as the chances might be, the receiving team might actually be able to score by running the ball back for a touchdown, as Dan "Will-o'-the-Wisp" Rhodes had done so long ago.

The game clearly had to be completed. No one would argue with that. The problem with continuing this particular game, however, was that after Clearview managed the two-point conversion, delirious Catamount fans poured out of the stands and onto the field without paying much attention to the clock.

Some of the fans swarmed the players, while others tried to pull down the goalpost. Still others hoisted up a dazed Jasper Knowles onto their shoulders and paraded him back and forth in front of the Catamount bench. The officials blew their whistles and tried to control the crowd, but they were having no more luck than before.

"Is that Lawton headed for the ambulance?" Ivy

asked. "You'd better get down there before he runs over somebody."

Rhodes had hoped at first that this time the crowd might settle down on its own, but it was clear within seconds that that just wasn't going to happen. He walked out of the stands and jogged toward the end zone, getting there just as Lawton reached the ambulance. The driver was nowhere around.

"Prob'ly gone for another hot dog," Lawton said. "Never did know a fella to eat so much at a football game."

"The band boosters need the money," Rhodes said. "You don't need to drive on the field this time. Just turn on the siren. Maybe that'll do the trick."

"It better do it quick, or those folks'll have the goalpost down on the ground," Lawton said.

Rhodes looked at the goalpost. There were several men standing on the crossbar, holding onto the uprights and rocking the post back and forth, while others were at the support pole, pushing against it and giving all the help they could to the men up on the crossbar.

"I'll take care of that," Rhodes told Lawton. "You just run the siren."

Two of the men jumped off the crossbar when they saw Rhodes coming. Then the siren wailed, and the crowd at the base began to scatter. Practically everyone had run off in one direction or another by the time Rhodes got there, and the others quickly followed. They didn't want to get arrested. The goalpost was still standing, though it might have been listing a bit to the left. That was good enough for Rhodes.

Rhodes turned toward the middle of the field, and he was gratified to see that Ruth Grady was already there. She had managed to get the fans to put Coach Knowles down, and had even made some headway with the mob surrounding the players in the middle of the field. Rhodes went to help her out, and before too long they had everyone at least backed up to the fence, if not back in the grandstand.

The players eventually calmed down enough to get the kickoff teams on the field, but the rest of the game was anticlimactic. After the obligatory delay-of-the-game penalty, the Clearview kicker squibbed the ball on the ground, and a Greyhound picked it up on the twenty-yard line. He ran to the left, avoided a couple of tacklers, circled back to the right, and then, as time expired, was overrun by half the Clearview team.

Yet another giddy celebration began, but Rhodes didn't feel like stopping this one. If the goalpost was pulled down, the school district would just have to buy a new one. What Rhodes was worried about now was the victory celebrations that were sure to ensue. He was afraid that it was going to be a long night.

RHODES COULD REMEMBER a time when the Clearview business district would have been humming on the Saturday morning after a game, but that had been a long time ago, before Wal-Mart had been built on the outskirts of town.

Now most of the downtown businesses were quiet, many of them practically deserted. The only real signs of life were outside the stores, where the Clearview cheerleaders were busy washing last week's spirit slogans from the windows and replacing them with new ones.

One window they hadn't gotten to yet depicted some kind of dog—which, Rhodes supposed, represented the Garton mascot—impaled on a spit above a roaring fire. Under the flames the words GRILL THE GREYHOUNDS were painted in blue and gold. It wasn't going to be easy to top that one.

Rhodes was headed to Billy Lee's drugstore, the only place that had a crowd of any kind inside. That was because Lee's was the gathering spot for an informal group known as the Catamount Club, composed of the team's biggest boosters, mostly local businessmen who had been waiting for years for something like the previous evening's game. The membership had varied over time, but some of the men had been coming to the drugstore for decades.

They were in the back of the shop when Rhodes arrived, sitting around a rickety wooden table that was located just to the left of the high counter that separated the pharmacy from the rest of the store. There were cigarette burns on the edge of the table, but they weren't recent. None of the men smoked now, though several of them had in the past. There was a thirty-cup coffeepot on a smaller table, and each of the Catamount Clubbers had his own mug with his name painted on it in blue and gold.

Ron Tandy, a real estate agent, was the leader of the group. He had been one of the founding members, and he was one of the few people in town who still remembered Rhodes's Will-o'-the-Wisp days.

He had a fringe of white hair around his head, watery blue eyes, and smooth pink cheeks. The other men at the table were Tom Fannin, who owned a couple of convenience stores; Gerald Bonny, a lawyer; Jimmy Bedlow, who managed Bedlow's Department Store; and Clyde Ballinger, the director of Clearview's largest funeral home. Jerry Tabor wasn't there, though Rhodes knew he was a regular.

Billy Lee, the owner of the drugstore, oversaw the whole thing from behind the counter. He never had much to say, but he heard everything that went on.

The center of attention was, of course, Jasper Knowles, and Rhodes arrived just in time to hear Tandy ask him what was on everyone's mind. "Why did Meredith take that punch at you, Coach?"

"Yeah, what was that all about?" Tom Fannin asked. Fannin was about forty, his hair just beginning to go gray at the temples.

Clyde Ballinger looked up and saw Rhodes. "Wait a minute, fellas. Here's the law. You want some coffee, Sheriff?"

Rhodes declined. He wasn't a coffee drinker. He preferred Dr. Pepper at any time of the day or night.

"Well, pull up a chair," Ballinger said. "You might be interested in this."

Rhodes sat down and waited for Knowles to answer. The coach looked uncomfortable. He took a sip of coffee and looked around at the group of men at the table.

"I don't know much about it," he finally said.

"You don't expect us to believe that," Bedlow

said. "You were there. You were the one he took a swing at."

Bedlow was a snappy dresser, even on Saturday morning, but then he managed a department store. He was wearing a pair of gray no-iron Dockers, black Rockport loafers with tassels, and a white shirt with a button-down collar. Most of the other men had on jeans and casual shirts, except for Ballinger, who was wearing a suit. He was always wearing a suit. Rhodes sometimes wondered if he slept in one.

"You might as well believe it," Knowles said. "It was sort of crazy down there."

"What do you mean, *crazy?*" Gerald Bonny asked, as if he expected Knowles to supply some kind of legally acceptable definition.

"I mean crazy," Knowles said, setting his cup on the table. "Brady was acting crazy, and then he tried to hit me."

"There's crazy, and then there's crazy," Tandy said. "We still don't know what you mean."

"I mean Brady didn't seem to know what the hell was goin' on out there. Maybe it was all the excitement, or maybe he just lost it, but he was tryin' to get me to send in the kickin' team."

There was a moment of stunned silence as the men absorbed the enormity of what Knowles had said.

Billy Lee leaned over the pharmacy counter and broke the silence. "You mean he wanted to kick the point instead of going for two when we were behind in penetrations? But that's crazy!"

"That's what I've been tryin' to tell you!" Knowles looked around the table. "And that's why he punched me, I guess. I wouldn't call for the kicker.

I was goin' for the two all the way. Maybe Brady thought I was goin' to lose the game for us. Maybe he thought *we* were ahead in penetrations, but he should've known better. Frankie was keepin' the stats, and he had it all down."

Frankie was Knowles's son, the third-string quarterback. He was a fixture on the bench. He always carried a clipboard, and he never got into the games.

"So Brady punched you because he thought you were going to lose the game," Clyde Ballinger said. "I guess that makes sense."

"Maybe it does," Bedlow said. "But I'm not so sure. Where is Brady, anyway? He's usually here on Saturdays."

"Maybe he was embarrassed," Tandy said. "I damn sure would be if I'd pulled a stunt like that. You going to fire his ass, Coach?"

"Well, I don't know about that," Knowles said. "Brady's a good man with an offense. If he apologizes, I guess there's no harm done. Lord knows, there's been times when I wanted to throw a punch at him when some play he sent in didn't work."

"But you never did," Ballinger said. "Did you?"

"Lord no. I wouldn't do a thing like that."

"And that's the point," Ballinger said. "Brady should've known better."

Knowles wasn't so sure. "Like I said, we'll have to talk it over. I expect he'll apologize, and then we'll see."

"What about that fight after Jay Kelton tackled that Garton kid?" Fannin asked. "I heard on the radio station when I was coming over here that the Garton coaches are really hacked off about their player gettin' kicked out, too. They say they're gonna get some kinda restrainin' order and then sue to have the refs' decision overturned and get their boys in the district game instead of us.''

Rhodes hadn't heard that little bit of news, and apparently no one else had, either.

''Those coaches ought to be ashamed,'' Gerald Bonny said. ''Taking something like that to court. The game's supposed to be played on the field, not in a courtroom.''

''Right,'' Fannin said. ''A courtroom's where you get those million-dollar whiplash lawsuits.''

Bonny was insulted. ''I don't do that kind of work.''

''If those Garton coaches take us to court, are you going to represent our side of things?'' Bedlow asked him.

''Damn right. That's different. I won't charge a dime. You can count on me, Coach.''

''A lawyer taking a case for free?'' Ballinger said. ''Now I've heard everything.''

The phone in the pharmacy rang, and Lee answered it. He listened a second and said, ''It's for you, Sheriff.''

Rhodes got up and went to the counter. Lee handed him the phone.

It was Hack Jensen. ''You better get over here, Sheriff,'' he said. ''We got us a little trouble.''

''What kind of trouble?''

''Buddy Reynolds has found a dead man. Says it's Brady Meredith.''

''I'm on my way.''

FOUR

IF BLACKLIN COUNTY'S jailer looked like Lou Costello, the dispatcher looked like Bud Abbott. He was sitting at his desk by the radio when Rhodes walked into the jail office. The little Mega Watchman TV set was tuned to "The Price Is Right," but Hack wasn't watching it.

"All right," Rhodes said. "What's this about a dead man?"

"I told you," Hack said. "Buddy says it's Brady Meredith. That don't mean it is, but Buddy wouldn't say it if he wasn't pretty sure he was right."

That was true. Buddy had his faults as a deputy, but saying things out of turn wasn't one of them.

"Besides," Hack said, "the body's in a car. I checked the license plate on our computer, and it matches Meredith's. Computer's a right handy thing to have around the office for things like that."

"I know," Rhodes said.

He didn't want to get into an argument about technology with Hack, who had argued for years that the county was far behind the rest of the world as far as keeping up with the latest scientific advances went.

"And another thing," Hack said.

"What?"

"Nancy Meredith called right after Buddy did. Said that Brady didn't come home after the game.

Wanted to know if we'd heard anything about an accident, which of course we ain't. I didn't say anything about Buddy's call or the car with the body in it."

"Where's the car?" Rhodes asked.

"Down behind the football field. You know those trees by that little creek? Couple of kids were down there huntin' with their BB guns and ran across the car. They saw somebody in it and got worried when he didn't move, so they told their mamas, and their mamas called me. I sent Buddy."

"Did he call you on the radio after he got there?"

Hack gave Rhodes a look. "You mean did it go out over the air about Brady Meredith bein' dead so ever'body that has a scanner could hear about it?"

"I'm sorry," Rhodes said. "I should have known better than to ask."

"You sure as shootin' should've. Soon's he called in, we switched to a private channel."

Rhodes was glad they'd remembered to do it. When the news got out, there was going to be a sensation. He hadn't mentioned anything about it to the members of the Catamount Club before he left the drugstore, not because they wouldn't find out but because there was no need to upset them if the body turned out not to be Brady's.

"I'd better get down there," Rhodes said. "Has everybody been called?"

This time, Hack didn't even bother to answer. He just shook his head sadly.

"Sorry again," Rhodes said. "I'll call after Buddy and I look over the scene."

"Figgered you would," Hack said.

WHEN THE NEW high school had been built on the edge of town ten years earlier, the football stadium had been located on the other side of Clearview. The school board had looked into the cost of a new stadium and had discovered that it would be cheaper to move the old one to the new school.

The stands had been dismantled, moved, and reassembled, so that the stadium now looked exactly as it had when Rhodes had been playing for the Catamounts. Seeing it in its new location was always a little disorienting, however.

The nearby high school building was of course very different from the one Rhodes had attended. It was big and low and had very few windows. The lack of windows was no doubt conducive to lower heating and cooling bills and therefore a wise economic choice, but Rhodes was pretty sure he would have gone crazy if he'd had to attend classes in a building with no windows. The old building had been hot in the fall and spring and cold in the winter, but at least you could look out the window if you got bored.

The stadium sat across an unpaved parking lot and down a little hill from the high school building. The town of Clearview hadn't grown out to the school quite yet, though there were a few houses across the road. Behind the stadium, however, there were open fields and a thick stand of trees along a little creek that ran south for about a quarter of a mile and then more or less disappeared. There was seldom any water in the creek, and even when there was, it barely covered the ground.

Rhodes drove past the stadium with hardly a thought about the previous night's game. There was no road from the parking lot into the fields, though there was a rutted path where someone, probably one of the fields' owners, occasionally drove into them.

Rhodes followed the ruts, the county car bouncing a little on the rough ground. He could see a white car down among the trees, and there was something darker beyond it, probably the car the body was in.

Rhodes stopped and got out when he reached Buddy's car. A front had come through early in the morning, and the day was chilly, gray and overcast, with a heavy mist hanging in the air and among the limbs of the trees. Moisture dripped off the dead leaves. From farther away, a crow called and then was quiet.

"What have we got, Buddy?" Rhodes asked.

Buddy Reynolds was standing next to the dark-colored car, which was a navy blue Taurus. All the windows were up, but Rhodes could see that someone was inside, slumped over the steering wheel. It looked like Meredith, all right. Whoever it was had been shot in the right side of the head. There was blood on the driver's window.

"Dead man in the front seat," Buddy said. Buddy was a lean man with a narrow face that made him look meaner than he was. "Looks like Brady Meredith to me."

"Have you touched anything?"

"Not a thing. I've been waitin' for you. 'Course

those kids trampled all over the grass around here. Be hard to tell if there's been anybody else around.''

Rhodes shivered as a drop of cold water fell from a tree and hit him on the cheek. He brushed it off and said, ''What about the car?''

''It's Brady's car. Hack checked it out on the computer.''

''I know. I meant have you looked it over.''

Buddy nodded. ''Just from the outside, though. I thought I'd better wait on you.''

''All right, then. Let's get to it.''

THE INSPECTION TOOK them most of the morning, and they didn't find much. There were no fingerprints on the passenger-side door handle. Someone had wiped it, along with most of the interior of the car.

''Somebody was in there with him,'' Buddy said. ''Must've been somebody he knew. Wonder how he got away?''

''Could have walked,'' Rhodes said. ''Could have had a car parked nearby. Hard to say.''

There were no other car tracks, however.

''Probably parked right up there by the stadium,'' Buddy said. ''Wonder how many cars were up there last night?''

Rhodes didn't know. It didn't matter. They'd never be able to tell which one the killer had been in. Unless there were some sort of tracks to follow back up to the parking lot.

But there weren't. The mist in the air was all the rain they'd had for quite a while, and the ground was hard as a sidewalk.

"Too bad it didn't come a good hard shower last night," Buddy said. "We might've found some tracks if it had."

"We'll look anyway," Rhodes said, knowing that it was probably useless.

Even if they found tracks, it would most likely be impossible to distinguish between any signs the boys had made and those the killer might have left. Sherlock Holmes would have probably found a couple of heel marks and been able to tell them everything but the killer's hair color, but Holmes wasn't one of Rhodes's deputies.

They looked for nearly an hour, finding nothing, then vacuumed the car on the off chance that they might turn up some kind of fiber, some kind of dirt, some minute scrap of paper—anything that would give them a lead to the killer.

Rhodes didn't have much faith in that kind of evidence, though. He depended more on talking to people and sifting through their stories, on finding out the possible motives and trying to discover who had the best one, on doggedly keeping after people until someone cracked.

But he knew the value of being thorough, so they did the scene properly, took photographs, and bagged everything that looked remotely suspicious, such as the cigarette butt in the car's ashtray. They didn't try to go through Meredith's clothing. Rhodes would do that later, at the funeral home.

It took them three hours to go over everything. When they were finished, they didn't know much more than when they'd begun.

They knew that Brady Meredith was dead, shot in the head. Rhodes estimated that the bullet had been fired by a small-caliber gun, maybe a .32, but they'd have to wait to know for sure. The bullet was still in Brady's head.

"Probably knew the guy," Buddy said. "Otherwise he wouldn't let him in the car with him."

"Are you sure it was a guy?" Rhodes asked.

"Car shut up like that, all the windows up, if it was a woman, you could still smell the perfume."

Rhodes wasn't so sure. "Some women don't wear perfume. Besides, the car smells like smoke. That would cover up any perfume smell."

Buddy didn't approve of smoking. "Football coaches oughtn't to smoke."

"Maybe he didn't. That's why we put that butt in a bag."

"Probably half the smokers in the county smoke Marlboros."

"Probably."

"Yeah. You ready for me to call the J.P. and the ambulance?"

"I guess you might as well."

"Who's gonna tell Brady's wife?"

"I'll see about that," Rhodes said.

RHODES DIDN'T GO to Meredith's house immediately. He drove over to the high school building and parked by the gym where he knew Jasper Knowles would be by now, watching the video from last night's game with the assistant coaches. Except for Brady Meredith, of course. They would analyze the video and then the next day bring in the team to go over it in the field house.

The entrance to the gym had a big sign over the double doors, painted in blue and gold on a white background: the image of a bobcat's head over the words YOU'RE ENTERING CATAMOUNT COUNTRY!

Rhodes went inside and was immediately struck by the fact that it smelled exactly the same as the gym at the old high school he had attended, a peculiar mixture of sweat, mildew, and wet socks.

The coaching offices were in the back of the gym, and Rhodes walked around the edge of the basketball court, remembering the admonitions of every gym teacher he'd ever had never to walk on the floor of the court wearing street shoes. His shoes had rubber soles, but despite that, he couldn't overcome his old conditioning.

There were several doors at the back of the gym, all of them with blue and gold slogans painted above them: THE ONLY PEOPLE WHO FAIL ARE THOSE WHO FAIL TO TRY! NO GUTS, NO GLORY! and NO FEAR. The third door led to the video room. Rhodes could hear voices inside.

"Damn, Jasper, I believe that Garton boy *was* out of bounds when Kelton hit him. Run that back and freeze it, Bob."

Rhodes entered the room and stood silently by the door to watch the play again, and when the picture froze it showed clearly that the Garton runner's feet had both been out of bounds before he was tackled. Not far out, mind you, but certainly far enough.

"Damn. Reckon that'll help 'em with that pissant lawsuit, Jasper?"

"Don't know, Roy," Knowles said. "But I doubt it. I talked some to Gerald Bonny about it this morning, and he said he'd never heard about any case where the courts overruled a referee. He said he'd look it up, though."

Roy Kenner was the defensive coach, a hard-featured man with dark, brush-cut hair. He was known as a tough disciplinarian who occasionally showed favoritism to players whose fathers had influence in the community. Rhodes didn't know whether the latter part was true, though he suspected that the first part certainly was.

"I wish Brady was here," Kenner said. "Where the hell is he, anyway?"

"Hiding his head in shame," another voice said. This one belonged to Bob Deedham, the special teams coach. "That's where I'd be if I'd swung at the coach."

Deedham was burly and wide, with shoulders that filled a doorway with ease. He was the only member of the Clearview coaching staff who'd played football after college. He'd spent a season with the Houston Oilers, though he'd never made it past the practice squad.

"Anybody see where he went after he made such an ass of himself?" Kenner asked.

"Nobody was looking," Deedham said. "We were all watching the field."

"Bet he got drunk," Kenner said. "I hear he drinks a bit."

"He didn't get drunk," Rhodes said from the doorway.

Roy Kenner nearly fell out of his chair. "Damn! Don't scare me like that. Who the hell's back there?"

Rhodes reached out and flipped the light switch. Overhead, fluorescent lights hummed, blinked, and then stayed on. Knowles, Deedham, and Kenner were sitting on wooden folding chairs in front of the big-screen TV set. Deedham had a remote control in his right hand. He punched the power button, turning off the VCR. The screen of the TV set filled with electronic snow.

"It's the sheriff," Deedham said, just in case that wasn't obvious to everyone. "What do you know about Brady?"

"I know where he is," Rhodes said. He wished there was an easy way to say what he had to tell them, but there wasn't. So he just said it. "He's dead."

Jasper Knowles stood up, knocking over his chair.

"Brady's dead? What the hell happened? Was he in a car wreck?"

"He wasn't in a car wreck." Rhodes went on to explain about the boys and the car and what had happened to Brady.

"It wasn't suicide, was it?" Deedham asked.

Rhodes said that he was pretty sure it wasn't. There was no weapon in the car, for one thing.

"That makes it murder, then," Deedham said.

Rhodes agreed that it was murder. There wasn't much doubt about it.

"Double damn," Kenner said, giving a sidelong

glance at Knowles. "Murder. Who'd want to shoot Brady?"

Deedham was more practical. "This is going to play hell with our preparation for that bi-district game with Springville next week."

"Good Lord, Bob," Knowles said. "How can you think about a football game when Brady's been killed?"

Deedham leaned back in his chair. "Easy. Brady's dead, but that Springville quarterback's not. He passed for nearly three hundred yards last night, and we have to get ready for him and all those sneaky little receivers he's got. That game's going to be played no matter what's happened to Brady, and you'd better get your mind on it."

"You never did like Brady much, did you?" Kenner said.

"You got that right," Deedham agreed. "He was sloppy. I didn't like the way he called a game, I didn't like the way he treated the players, and I didn't like it that he'd go drinking on the weekends. That's no way to behave if you're a coach."

"He knew how to run an offense," Knowles said.

Rhodes thought that was a pretty weak defense, and Deedham obviously didn't agree with it, but it seemed to be the only one that Knowles had. It was the same one he'd used at the drugstore.

"I was hoping you'd call your wife," Rhodes told the head coach. "She knows Nancy Meredith, doesn't she?"

"She knows her."

"What about your wives?" Rhodes asked the other coaches.

"Mine knows her pretty well," Kenner said.

"Mine too," Deedham said.

"I'm going to have to tell her about her husband," Rhodes said. "Maybe your wives could go over there and give her some comfort."

"That's a good idea," Knowles said. "We'll call them. Is there anything else we can do?"

"You can be thinking about who might have a motive to kill Meredith."

"You mean aside from Jasper?" Deedham said.

"Now what in the hell is that supposed to mean?" Kenner wanted to know.

"Just what I said. Jasper's the one Brady took a swing at, isn't he? And they haven't really gotten along all year."

"That doesn't mean I'd want to kill him," Knowles said. "It was just something that happened in the heat of the game."

Deedham shrugged. "If you say so."

Kenner walked over to Deedham's chair and stood over him. "Damn right he says so. And I say so. If anybody here didn't like Brady, it was you. You were always tryin' to undermine him with the team and with Jasper."

"I'm not the one who said he liked to drink a bit," Deedham pointed out. "That was you."

"I was jokin'."

"The hell you were."

Rhodes could have spoken up and stopped the argument, but he decided to let it run on. He thought he might learn something. Jasper Knowles wasn't interested in what Rhodes might learn, however.

"You two shut up," he told his assistants. "The sheriff's asked us to call our wives and have 'em go over to see Nancy, and that's what we're gonna do. Now you go phone, Roy."

Kenner walked off without saying anything else. Deedham sat and fiddled with the remote control.

"You want anything else from us, Sheriff?" Knowles asked.

"Not right now. I'll want to talk to all of you again, though. The players, too."

Deedham looked up. "You don't want to go upsetting our players, Sheriff. We've got a big game coming up in just about a week."

"Brady Meredith doesn't," Rhodes said. "He won't be there."

"He'll be there in spirit," Deedham said. He sat up straighter. "That's an idea, Jasper! We can dedicate the game to Brady. The kids'll be so fired up, we'll win in a walkover. Hell, we can dedicate the rest of the season to him! This could be our ticket to the championship!"

Rhodes didn't know Deedham very well, but he thought he could grow to dislike him without putting too much effort into it. He was about to say something, but Knowles beat him to it.

"We can't capitalize on Brady's death like that, Bob. It wouldn't be right. I don't want to win that bad."

"I do," Deedham said. "I don't like losing."

"Hardly anybody does," Knowles said. "But if

you don't win the right way, what good does it do you?''

Deedham gave a short, barking laugh. ''Nobody cares *how* you win, Jasper. As long as you've been coaching, you ought to know that. They just want you to win. I'll bet Rhodes finds that out before long.''

Rhodes had an uneasy feeling that Deedham was right.

FIVE

NANCY MEREDITH was nowhere near as big as her husband. She was a small-boned woman, about five-four, with mousy brown hair that hung to her shoulders. She didn't ask Rhodes in after he told her who he was. She just stood and looked at him.

Finally she said, "Was there an accident?"

"No," Rhodes said. "Do you mind if I come in?"

"Oh. No. Of course not."

She stepped back into the house, opening the door wider. Rhodes went inside, and she closed it behind him very quietly.

"We can go in the kitchen," she said.

That was fine with Rhodes. Maybe the kitchen was where she was most comfortable. He followed her down a short hall, through the den and into the kitchen, which was also the dining area. There was a chrome table with a yellow Formica top and four matching chairs. A cut-glass salt-and-pepper set sat in the middle of the table.

"Would you like some coffee?" she asked.

Rhodes declined. "I have to talk to you about Brady," he said.

Nancy pulled out one of the chairs and sat down. "He's hurt, isn't he? That's why you're here."

"I'm afraid it's worse than that," Rhodes said. "He's dead."

She didn't faint or scream or even start crying. She just sat there and looked up at Rhodes as if she were expecting him to say more.

He waited until she asked, "How did it happen?"

"Somebody shot him," Rhodes told her.

She shook her head. "A hunting accident? Brady didn't even like to go hunting."

"It wasn't an accident. Somebody shot him deliberately."

"Who?"

"I don't know that yet," Rhodes said. "I was hoping that you might be able to give me some idea."

"How could I? Do you think I did it?"

Rhodes didn't think that, but it was always a possibility.

"I thought you might know if there was anyone who might have reason to want him dead," he said. "Does he have any enemies? Has anybody been threatening him?"

"No. Everybody likes Brady." She clenched her hands in her lap. "He never got any threats, even last year when the team wasn't playing so well. Is this a joke?"

"I wouldn't joke about something like this," Rhodes said.

"Brady likes playing jokes, but this isn't very funny."

"I wish it were a joke, but it's not. I'm sorry. Brady's dead. Someone killed him."

Nancy Meredith started crying then, putting her face in her hands to hide the tears. Rhodes didn't have a handkerchief to offer her, but there was a roll of paper towels sitting by the sink. He tore one off the roll and handed it to her. It was all he could do. He was glad to hear the doorbell ring, knowing that one or more of the other coaches' wives had arrived.

NELSON "GOOBER" VANCE was the sports reporter for the Clearview *Herald*. Because the *Herald* could afford only one reporter, he was also the society writer, the feature writer, and the front-page columnist ("Around the Town with Goob"). But his heart was with the Catamounts. Rhodes figured that if anyone knew about Brady Meredith, it was Vance, so when he left Nancy Meredith, he went to the newspaper office.

Rhodes could remember a time when the newspaper office had a smell as distinctive as the gym, a smell made up of printer's ink and hot machinery and paper. And the sound of the press was a constant hum.

It wasn't like that now. It could have belonged to an insurance agent or a real estate salesman. There were four desks, each one with a computer terminal sitting on it. There was a big stack of back issues on one desk, along with some forms for classified ads. The other desks were covered with note pads and papers.

The only person in the office was Goober Vance. He was sitting at his desk, typing on a computer keyboard. Or maybe he wasn't typing, since he wasn't using a typewriter. Rhodes wasn't sure what the right word was.

"Just a second, Sheriff," Vance said. A toothpick

waggled at the corner of his mouth. He had quit smoking a year or so ago and had since contributed mightily to deforestation. "Have a seat. Be with you soon's I finish this paragraph."

Rhodes sat at one of the vacant desks. Vance stared at the words appearing on his computer monitor, typed a period with a flourish, and looked over at the sheriff.

"Now, then, what can I do for you?" he asked.

"Tell me a little about Brady Meredith," Rhodes said.

"Funny you should want to know about him," Vance said. He was a small man with wavy brown hair and small brown eyes that were a little too close together. "I was just writing an article about his death."

"What were you saying?"

"I was saying that it was a shame that a young and successful coach had to die in such a bizarre way. You want to fill me in on that?"

Rhodes wasn't surprised that Vance already knew about Meredith's murder. It was almost impossible to keep a secret in a small town like Clearview.

"You probably already know as much as I do. What I want to find out is what's not going into the article."

Vance removed the gnawed toothpick from his mouth and looked at it for a moment before tossing it into a green metal trash can beside his desk. He reached into his shirt pocket and took out a plastic box, removed a toothpick, and stuck it between his teeth.

"You mean about his private life?" he asked after working the toothpick from the right side of his mouth to the left.

"I mean about his drinking and anything else that might give me some idea about how he wound up dead."

"He drank a little, but not enough to make a difference to anybody. Everybody needs a beer now and then, Sheriff, just to relax. He was discreet about it."

That was all that mattered. The Clearview school board didn't care how teachers conducted their personal lives as long as their personal lives were kept private and didn't affect their performance in the classroom.

"*Where* he drank, now, that's something else," Vance said.

"Where did he drink?" Rhodes asked.

"He had to get out of town, so not too many people would see him. He went out to The County Line. I wouldn't go there, myself."

Rhodes resisted asking Vance where he would go. He said, "That's a pretty rough place. We've had a few calls about it."

"I know. I write the 'Law and Order' column." He was referring to a weekly column that gave readers a condensed version of the various crimes and arrests throughout the county. "You ever read that?"

"I don't need to," Rhodes pointed out.

"Right. Well, from what I hear, most of the stuff that happens out there at The County Line never gets reported to you. The people involved are the kind that like to settle things themselves."

True enough. The emergency room of the Clearview Hospital had a few cases every weekend that came from The County Line, though the patients usually said something like, "I fell off my bike," or "I slipped in the tub." While the former excuse was at least likely, the latter was clearly false. Most of the people who made that claim didn't look as if they'd been near a bathtub for several weeks.

"Did Meredith ever get in any fights out there?" Rhodes asked.

"Not that I've heard about. There are plenty of rough customers out there, though. Wonder if any of them had a lot of money bet on the game last night?"

Rhodes thought about Hayes Ford. And he thought about the fight between Meredith and Jasper Knowles. Meredith had wanted to kick the point instead of going for two. Could that mean that Meredith was aware of some sort of bet on the game? Or could Meredith himself have made a bet? It didn't seem likely, but anything was possible.

"What about Meredith?" Rhodes asked. "Do you think he might have bet with someone?"

Vance gave it some thought. "Maybe. But if he did, I didn't know about it."

Vance seemed to believe he knew most of what went on, but if Meredith had been betting on the team, he would have kept it very quiet.

Vance changed the subject. "And then there's Meredith's wife," he said.

"What about her?" Rhodes asked.

"Kind of drab for the wife of a big-time football coach, wouldn't you say?"

Rhodes hadn't really thought about that, but it was obvious that there was more to the story. It was also obvious that Vance was going to tell him about it.

"Brady married her when they were in college. She was a cheerleader then, but she's lost a little spark in the years since. Brady thought he could do better."

"Who with? Anybody I should know about?"

"You catch on quick, Sheriff." The toothpick danced. "No wonder you're such an effective lawman."

Rhodes couldn't tell whether Vance was paying him a compliment or being sarcastic.

Vance said, "Ever seen Bob Deedham's wife?"

Rhodes said that he hadn't. Velma Knowles had been the one ringing Nancy Meredith's doorbell.

"Name's Terry. Now there's somebody who still looks like a cheerleader. Blonde, big hair, big eyes, big pom-poms. The works. The kind of woman that Meredith would go for."

Rhodes wasn't sure how to take the "pom-poms" remark, but he didn't ask for clarification. Deedham's attitude was beginning to make more sense than it had earlier.

"And there's one other thing," Vance said.

Rhodes waited.

"Did you notice anything about the team last night? Did they seem especially aggressive to you?"

"They were fired up, all right," Rhodes said.

"There've been some rumors about that," Vance said. He took out his toothpick and replaced it with a fresh one. "You might have heard them."

"No. I'm always the last one to hear rumors."

Vance looked as if he doubted that, then shrugged. "Maybe so. What do you think could hop up a team like that?"

"I'm not very good at guessing," Rhodes said. "Why don't you tell me."

"Steroids," Vance said. "Ever hear about them?"

Rhodes had heard about them, all right. "You say it's just a rumor?"

"But worth checking out. Steroids can do funny things to a kid. If one got mad enough, he might even shoot his coach."

"Would any of them have a reason to do that?"

"They wouldn't need much of a reason. Let's say someone identified pretty strongly with the head coach and you took a poke at him. That might be enough. It's worth checking out."

Rhodes agreed that it was. "Do you have anything else for me?"

"That's about it," Vance said. "I'd think that was enough to give you a start."

It was more than enough. Vance was a veritable Geraldo when it came to dishing the dirt. Rhodes had plenty to think about: The County Line, Hayes Ford, Bob Deedham's wife (not to mention Deedham himself), and steroids.

"You know that this is the kind of stuff that'll never get in the paper, don't you?" Goober asked.

Rhodes knew it. The Clearview newspaper's editorial policy was one that advocated praising local politicians whenever possible, boosting the local economy by running free "shop at home in Clearview'' ads when space permitted, letting everyone know whose aunt from Dallas was in town for a visit, giving generous space to all weddings and funerals, supporting the football team, and ignoring anything at all that might make Clearview look anything less than the most idyllic place to live in the state of Texas.

Goober continued, ''But that doesn't mean I wouldn't like to know the outcome of all this. I may not be able to write it, but I like to know what's going on around town anyway.''

''If there's anything I think you should know, you'll hear from me,'' Rhodes said, not so sure that he wanted to give Vance anything more to gossip about. He thanked the reporter for his time and stood up. ''And if you hear of anything else that might help me, let me know.''

''You can count on me, Sheriff,'' Vance said. ''Always glad to cooperate with the Law.''

He was already turning back to the monitor before Rhodes was out the door.

HACK AND LAWTON were deep in conversation when Rhodes walked in the jailhouse. They looked up expectantly but didn't say anything, which was a bad sign. Rhodes thought it might be easier just to ignore them. He put the cigarette butt in the evidence locker, which was really just an old black safe, then sat at his desk, put on his reading glasses, and started doing the paperwork on the Meredith death.

''He ain't gonna talk to us,'' Hack said behind his back. ''Too busy, I guess.''

"Sure," Lawton said. "I save his life at the game last night and then he slights me. That's the thanks I get."

Rhodes swiveled around and looked at them. "I appreciate it that you saved my life," he told Lawton. "And I'm not too busy to talk if there's anything to talk about. Is there?"

"We thought you might want to tell us if it was Brady Meredith in that car or not," Hack said. "And then you might ask if there's anything else goin' on around here that you oughta know about."

Rhodes sighed and took his glasses off. "It was Meredith, all right. Somebody shot him. I don't know who it was yet."

"You oughta talk to that Goober Vance down at the paper," Lawton said. "He knows ever'thing that goes on with that football team."

"I talked to him. He had a lot of hints, but no real facts. I'll have to find those out myself."

"That figgers," Hack said. "I expect you'll be gettin' a lot of hints, considerin' how interested everybody is in gettin' this murder solved and out of the way so the really important stuff can go on as usual."

"What important stuff?" Rhodes asked.

"Football," Lawton said. "That's what all the calls have been about."

"Calls? Nobody mentioned any calls."

"That's 'cause you were so busy when you came in," Hack said. "You didn't ask about any calls, so I didn't mention 'em. Didn't want to bother you, seein' as how you were so busy."

"Tell me about the calls," Rhodes said.

"There was a lot of 'em," Hack said. "Seems like ever'body in town already knows for sure that Brady's dead. Except me and Lawton, of course. Nobody told us. Not until we asked, anyway."

"But I told you then," Rhodes said, wanting to get on with it. "What about the calls?"

"Like Hack told you," Lawton said. "There was a lot of 'em. Phone like to rung off the hook."

Rhodes slipped his glasses in his shirt pocket. Hack and Lawton were always that way. It took forever for them to get to the point. Rhodes was used to it, and he knew there was no way to hurry them.

He tried, however. "What were the calls about?"

"Football," Lawton said. "I told you that."

"That's right," Hack said. "He did."

"What about football?"

"About how they want this taken care of immediately," Hack said.

"If not sooner," Lawton added.

"You got a call from the mayor," Hack said, looking at a note pad. "And two from the county commissioners, and one from the high school principal. Then you got about twenty more from just your ordinary citizens."

"And they want the murder solved today," Rhodes said.

"That'd be nice," Hack said. "But tomorrow'd be OK. Just as long as it's taken care of quick and doesn't interfere with the game next Saturday. They had some suggestions for you, too, about where to start lookin' and all."

"And where was that?"

"Garton," Lawton said. "Lots of folks say it musta been somebody from Garton that was sore about the win. Like that lady with her hair and face dyed. You remember her?"

Rhodes said that he did.

"Well, she'd hafta be crazy to paint herself up like that. So maybe she was crazy enough to kill somebody. You know about that lawsuit?"

"I've heard about it," Rhodes said.

"Well, don't that prove they're crazy?"

Rhodes wasn't sure. "Maybe they'll win."

Lawton snorted. "No way. Judge'll throw it out in a New York minute. If they got away with that, half the schools in the state'd be goin' to court after every game, tryin' to get bad calls overturned. It'll never fly."

Rhodes had to admit that Lawton had a point, but before he could say so, the phone rang.

"Prob'ly another call about the game," Lawton said as Hack answered it.

"If it is, just say I'm not here," Rhodes said.

"Sheriff's not here," Hack said after listening for a few seconds. "He's out workin' on the case right now. But I'll be sure to tell him what you said."

He hung up. "That wasn't exactly what you thought it was gonna be."

"What was it, then?" Lawton asked. "Sure sounded like somebody callin' about the case."

"You ought not to listen in on official business," Hack told him. "You're just the jailer."

"I guess you think the jailer ain't just as official as you are. I guess you think—"

Rhodes cut in. "Never mind that right now. What was that call about, Hack?"

"That was Miz Wilkie," he said. "Your old sweetie."

Mrs. Wilkie had never been Rhodes's "sweetie," though she had certainly been interested in him before his marriage to Ivy. Rhodes had done his best to avoid her then, and he didn't go out of his way to see her now, though occasionally he had to in the course of his job. She was working for James Allen, one of the county commissioners, as a secretary.

"What did she want?" Rhodes asked.

"Maybe she just wanted to see you again," Lawton said. "I bet you don't drop in on her very often these days."

Rhodes ignored him. "Hack? What did she want?"

"She wants to talk to you. But it's not about the murder. Or maybe it is."

"What did she say?" Rhodes asked.

Hack gave him a lopsided grin. "She said she's been hearin' motorsickles."

SIX

BEFORE GOING TO SEE Mrs. Wilkie, Rhodes drove to the funeral home. He'd missed lunch, and he would have liked to go home for a bologna sandwich, but Ivy insisted on buying low-fat bologna, which Rhodes suspected was made from turkey and which didn't taste like real bologna even if it wasn't. She also bought low-fat Miracle Whip, which didn't taste like much of anything. So Rhodes didn't figure he was missing much by skipping the meal. At least his waistline was shrinking a little.

He could have slipped by the new McDonald's and gotten something satisfyingly full of fat grams, but he didn't really have the time. He wanted to do as much as he could in as short a time as possible. It wouldn't be long before Hack couldn't hold off all the callers. They'd be calling him at home, at the jail, and anywhere else they thought he might be.

Clyde Ballinger was in his office in the small building in back of the funeral home proper, sitting at his desk, surrounded by the old paperbacks that he liked to read and collect, but he wasn't reading one when Rhodes walked in. He was looking at an issue of *Texas Football*.

"Did you know that Garton was picked to win state this year?" he asked, dropping the magazine on his desk.

Rhodes said that he'd known that. It had been in every article Goober Vance wrote about the team for the past week.

"Yeah, I guess you're right. But we beat them. I figure that means we're the favorites for the title now. That is, we are if we don't let this business with Brady distract us."

Rhodes had noticed that a lot of sports fans talked the way Ballinger did when referring to the teams they supported. It was never "they." It was always "we," as if the speaker were actually suiting up, taking the field, and playing in the games.

"How did the Catamount Club take the news?" Rhodes asked.

"I don't know. We didn't hear about it at the drugstore, and I haven't heard from any of them since we left. I don't expect they'll like it. Nobody will." He stood up. "You got any idea who did it, or why?"

"Not a one. Is Dr. White through with the body?"

"He sure is. He left a report for you. You want to go have a look at it?"

Rhodes said that would be a good idea, and the two of them went over to the funeral home. Before reading through the report, Rhodes looked through Meredith's clothing, but there was nothing there of any help. Just a wallet, a few coins, a pocket knife, and a comb.

The report had more useful information than the clothing. Meredith had been dead approximately ten hours, meaning that he'd been killed sometime around midnight. He'd been shot with a .32, and the bullet had been recovered. That was a bit of evidence that Rhodes could do a little checking on. He got the bullet, which Dr. White had bagged and tagged. Then he thanked Ballinger and started to leave.

"You ever read anything by Charles Williams?" Ballinger asked.

Rhodes hadn't, but he'd seen books by Williams in Ballinger's office.

"He wrote one about a football player that got mixed up in a murder," Ballinger said. "*A Touch of Death* is the name of it. You think any of our players are mixed up in this one?"

"I hope not," Rhodes said. "What do you think?"

"Football builds character," Ballinger said. "Those boys wouldn't have anything to do with something like this. Besides, they're just kids."

"Kids have killed before."

"Not this time," Ballinger said. "I'd bet on it."

"Speaking of betting," Rhodes said, "what can you tell me about Hayes Ford?"

Ballinger looked uncomfortable. There was no one else in the room with them, but he said, "Maybe we'd better go back to my office if we're going to talk about that."

BALLINGER DIDN'T SAY anything as they walked across the parking lot. When they were back in the office, Ballinger closed the door and walked behind his desk.

"Sit down, Sheriff," he said.

Rhodes sat on a couch and looked around at the books on Ballinger's shelves. Most of them had come from garage sales. You couldn't find the kind of books Ballinger liked in the stores.

"What did you ask me about Hayes Ford for?" Ballinger asked, sitting at his desk. "I hope you don't think I'd bet on a football game."

"I don't know about that," Rhodes said. "I know you've been in a card game or two."

Ballinger looked as if he might deny it and then thought better of it. "I've played poker once or twice. Just friendly games, here in town. Not with Ford, though. I don't even know if he plays cards. Anyway, there's nothing wrong with a friendly card game, is there?"

"Not unless you're gambling," Rhodes said. "Then it's against the law."

"Lots of things are against the law. Football pools, for one, but there's a football pool in every business in Clearview. At the high school, too, I bet. You haven't busted any of them, not that I've heard of."

"I haven't busted any of the card games, either, but I will if they get out of hand. That's not what I'm interested in, though. I'm interested in the betting on the football games. How much money do you think might be involved?"

There was a low rumble of thunder that shook the window panes in the office.

"Weather's not getting any better, is it?" Ballinger said. "I hear it might get colder tonight. Along with some rain that would be real miserable."

"Sure would," Rhodes agreed, though he wasn't interested in talking about the weather. "Now, you were just about to tell me your thoughts on the betting.''

Ballinger twisted around in his chair as if it were hurting his spine.

"I don't know that it would be a good idea to talk about that.''

"You and I have been friends for a long time,'' Rhodes said. "You know that you can trust me to keep a confidence. Nobody's going to know you said anything to me about this.''

"All right,'' Ballinger said, not sounding as if he really meant it. "How much do you know about Ford?''

"I've checked into him,'' Rhodes said. "We've tried to put a stop to the gambling before.''

"But you didn't catch him. He's one slick character, but you know that.''

"That's right. I know that. So tell me something I don't know. Like who bets with him. I almost caught him with someone last night, but I didn't get a good look at whoever it was.''

"I don't know who he bets with! Just because I've been in a card game or two doesn't mean I know all about the gambling in Blacklin County.''

"I thought that some of the card players might have mentioned Ford. Just in passing.''

"Maybe they have. But I can't tell you who they are.''

Rhodes knew that the Catamount Clubbers got together occasionally for cards and drinks. They were the ones that Ballinger played cards with, and Ballinger didn't want to incriminate his friends. Rhodes didn't really blame him.

There was another rumble of thunder and the first drops of rain began to fall.

"What about it?" Rhodes said.

Ballinger picked up the football magazine, dropped it, and said, "All right. I'll tell you what I know. But it isn't much."

"That doesn't matter. I just want to get an idea of some amounts. You don't have to name any names."

The rain started to fall harder. Rhodes could hear it splattering against the window panes.

"It could be pretty big money," Ballinger said, "if you added it all up. But I don't think anybody really bets all that much at one time."

Rhodes knew that already. Ford didn't take any big bets. Just a lot of small ones.

"Where do they bet?" Rhodes asked. "I know money changes hands at the games, but not a lot of it. The people we're talking about wouldn't be caught dead near Hayes Ford at a game."

"They sure wouldn't. Or anywhere else. Hayes runs a little book with an unlisted number he's got."

So that was it. Pretty simple when you thought about it. It might even be enough to put Ford out of business.

"How does he pay off and collect?"

"I don't know about that part of it. I don't bet, and I don't ask."

"But as far as you know, no one has made a large bet with him?"

"Not enough to kill anybody about, if that's what

you're getting at. Never more than forty or fifty dollars at a time. It's just in fun. But some people might bet a lot more. I wouldn't know. Anyway, I imagine Ford takes bets on lots of other games. Colleges, pros, basketball, too. It all adds up.''

Rhodes wondered if it all added up to murder. He stood up.

"Thanks, Clyde. I'm not going to mention this to anyone."

"I sure hope not," Ballinger said. "I'd never be able to go to the drugstore on Saturday morning again."

THE DRIVE TO the commissioner's office was cold and uncomfortable because Rhodes had gotten wet on his short jog from Ballinger's office to the county car. The rain continued to fall, sluicing across the windshield as the wipers whipped it aside.

The precinct office where Mrs. Wilkie worked was a long metal building, only the front part of which served as the commissioner's office. The back was a warehouse and garage for the heavy equipment used in keeping up the county roads in the precinct. Rhodes could see a bulldozer and a maintainer through the curtain of rain, as he trotted from his car to the office door.

Mrs. Wilkie looked up when he entered. Rain was dripping from his hair and running down the neck of his shirt. Without saying anything, Mrs. Wilkie opened a desk drawer and brought out a box of tissues. Rhodes pulled several from the box and dried his face. He thought that he'd be better off if he could bring himself to wear a Western-style hat, like every other sheriff in Texas.

"Thanks," he said when he was finished. He handed her the box.

"Certainly," she answered, putting the box back in the drawer.

She was always formal with him now that he was a married man, and she no longer dyed her hair the amazing shade of orangey red that it had once been. It was brown, with quite a bit of gray in it; she was at least ten years older than Rhodes, not that she would have admitted it. She was wearing a dark blue suit with a white blouse.

"Are you here about my telephone call?" she asked.

"That's right. I understand that you've heard motorcycles again."

The first time motorcycles had cropped up had been not so long ago, when Rhodes had been dealing with a man called Rapper. Rapper was still around somewhere, Rhodes supposed, though it hardly seemed probable that he would be back in Blacklin County. His first experience there hadn't turned out very well for him.

The only reason that Rhodes was visiting Mrs. Wilkie himself was that there might possibly be a connection between motorcycles and Brady Meredith. The County Line was about the only place nearby where bikers hung out, and then only when they were passing through. It was a tenuous connection, but Goober Vance had also mentioned steroids. Rapper was probably a lot of things, all of them un-

savory, but dealing in drugs was one of his special-
ties. If a coach wanted black-market steroids, Rapper
could no doubt supply them.

Besides, Rhodes thought, if Rapper had turned up
in Blacklin County again right at the time someone
had been murdered, that was suspicious in itself.
Rhodes didn't much believe in coincidence where
murder was concerned.

"I hear them at all hours of the night," Mrs.
Wilkie said. "It's a terrible racket. I can never get
back to sleep after they wake me up. I think they
must be hanging around at the Gottschalk place
again."

Rapper and his friend Nellie had been camping out
near a lake on their last visit to the county. They
might be there again, as unlikely as it seemed. It
wouldn't hurt to drive down there and look around.

"What about last night?" Rhodes asked.

"Oh, yes. I was at the game until about ten-thirty,
and I know you were there, too. I thought you handled things very well."

She gave Rhodes what she probably thought was
a coy look. He much preferred her formal approach.

"Thanks. I was just doing my job. What about the
motorcycles?"

"They came by late and woke me up. It was just
after one. I looked at the clock."

That would have given them plenty of time to have
been involved in killing Brady Meredith, assuming
that Dr. White's estimate of the time of death was
correct.

"I'll check it out," Rhodes said. "If they're still there, I'll see that they don't bother you anymore."

"I'd appreciate that. I need my beauty sleep."

Rhodes started to tell her that he was sure she did, but somehow that didn't seem like the right thing to say.

"I think it's just terrible about Coach Meredith," she went on. "Do you think these motorcycles have any connection to his death?"

Rhodes said that he wasn't sure. "But you never can tell."

"I know. That's why I called. Not just because I can't sleep, but because I remember the last time."

Rhodes thanked her for being a public-spirited citizen and turned to go.

Mrs. Wilkie called him back. "Mr. Allen wants to see you before you go. He's in his office."

Uh-oh, Rhodes thought. There could be only one reason that the commissioner wanted to see him, and he didn't really want to discuss Meredith's death with anyone right now. There was no way to avoid it, however.

"I'll just let him know you're here," Mrs. Wilkie said, picking up her telephone.

The door to Allen's office was just behind and to the right of Mrs. Wilkie's desk. Allen opened the door and motioned for Rhodes to come in.

When they were both inside and seated, he said, "What progress have you made on the Meredith killing?"

That was exactly what Rhodes had expected him

to ask, but that didn't mean he had a good answer for it.

"I'm looking into several things," he said, which he knew would be too vague to satisfy Allen.

And it was. He said, "What things?"

"Well, Mrs. Wilkie tells me that there's some chance Rapper's back in town. You might remember him."

"I remember, all right. Could he be mixed up in this?"

"It's a possibility. And there are several other people who may or may not be involved. I don't want to mention any names until I have more to go on."

"I can understand that. I don't want to put any pressure on you. But you know how important it is to get this cleared up, don't you? We can't have it affecting the team."

Rhodes could have told him that the team was already affected, but he didn't. Allen should be able to figure that out for himself.

"Winning district has brought this town together like nothing I've ever seen," Allen went on. "We can't have this murder tearing down what's been built."

Rhodes supposed that it was only natural for everyone to want to keep things running along as always, but at the same time he thought people should realize that murder wasn't something that you could just smooth over. It was quite likely that his investigation was going to involve a lot of people who would rather not be involved, and upset a lot of people that the commissioner would rather not upset.

"I'll do what I can to get it solved fast," Rhodes said, which was true. It was what he always did.

"That's good enough for me," Allen said.

Rhodes didn't believe him for a minute. What he really meant was "That's good enough for me just as long as the football team goes right on to the next game as if nothing has happened."

But something had happened. One of the coaches was dead, and Rhodes was going to have to talk to the players. Even if he didn't talk to them, they were naturally going to be affected.

There was no need for Rhodes to say any of that. Allen wouldn't like it, and it wouldn't do anyone any good.

"I appreciate your support," Rhodes said, and then he left.

RHODES STOPPED by the jail to tell Hack to get on his computer and see whether anyone in the county had bought a .32 pistol recently.

"Say, within the last couple of weeks. That might give us a place to start."

"Ever'body in Clearview already has a gun," Lawton pointed out. "Don't you watch TV? This is Texas."

Hack said, "Besides, people don't all buy their guns at Wal-Mart. They buy 'em at flea markets. If I was goin' to buy one, that's where I'd get it."

"I thought you liked using that computer of yours," Rhodes said.

"I'll check it out. I never said I wouldn't. You want me to send Ruth out there to the Gottschalk place to back you up? You always get in trouble when you don't get backup.''

''You can send her if she's not busy,'' Rhodes said, but he didn't really think he'd need her. He didn't even plan to get out of his car. How much trouble could he get in?

MRS. WILKIE LIVED in a little brick house in Milsby, a tiny community that had once been a town with its own school and post office and businesses. There was hardly a trace of it left now, just a few homes and some vacant buildings. The school was used as a community center when it was used at all.

Rhodes switched on his headlights as he drove by Mrs. Wilkie's house in the rain. It was only the middle of the afternoon, but the combination of the clouds and the rain made the day as dark as early evening. Rhodes thought that if Rapper were really camping out down by the lake, he'd be pretty wet by now.

Rhodes didn't like camping himself. He preferred the comforts of a real bed and central heat and air to sleeping on an inflatable mattress in the weather provided by nature. But if you were in Rapper's line of work, you didn't necessarily want to check into the nearest motel.

Rhodes turned off on a dirt road made slick by the rain. He drove slowly and carefully; it wouldn't do to slide off into the ditch that ran alongside the road. If he did, he wouldn't be able to get out by himself.

The turn into the Gottschalk property was marked by a cattle guard. There was no gate, and the cattle guard ratcheted under the tires as Rhodes drove across it.

He didn't relish the idea of driving down the rutted road that led to the lake. It was dangerously muddy and the rain was still falling. Even more embarrassing than sliding into the ditch would be getting stuck in the mud. However, he'd said he'd check on things, and it was too late to back out now. Besides, there was no place to turn around. That would mean getting off the road, and getting off the road, such as it was, would be even worse than staying on it.

So Rhodes kept on. The trick to driving in the mud was to keep going, slowly but steadily. If you stopped, you couldn't get any traction, and you were likely to dig yourself a hole that you couldn't get out of.

At the top of a little hill, Rhodes looked out over the lake, which of course wasn't really a lake at all but simply a large stock tank.

Because there hadn't been much rain for several months, the lake was not as large as it sometimes was. There was a sizable muddy margin between the bank and the water, which was being dimpled by the rain and riffled by the wind.

Down at the bottom of the hill near the lake, Rhodes saw the tents, two cheap one-man jobs probably bought at a discount store. The motorcycles were beside the tents with canvas covers thrown over them.

Sure enough, Rhodes thought. Rapper was back in town.

SEVEN

RHODES STARTED DOWN the hill. He was sorry that Mrs. Wilkie had been right about the motorcycles, since the presence of Rapper was going to complicate things considerably.

Or maybe not. Maybe he could tie the whole thing up in a neat package right now: Rapper killed Brady Meredith in an argument about the payment for steroids.

Somehow he didn't think it would be that easy, however.

When he got to the bottom of the hill, he looked around for a place to park. There was a wide, flat, grassy area near the tank dam about thirty yards from the tents. He didn't want to walk that far in the rain, but he didn't suppose he had much choice in the matter. Anyway, the rain seemed to be slowing down a bit.

Rhodes drove onto the grass, parked, and got out. The rain was no longer falling hard; it was more like a heavy mist in the air now, but it clung to his hair and soaked into his shirt and pants. The grass was so wet that cold water was squishing in his shoes by the time he'd walked halfway over to the tents. He told himself that if he ever bought himself a Western hat, he'd get some boots, too. Waterproof boots.

By the time Rhodes got near the tents, Rapper was

already standing in front of one of them looking at him.

Rhodes had never liked Rapper, because there had been nothing about him to like. He'd proved himself to be a congenital liar and a bully. He was short and pudgy, with his thinning hair greased straight back from a widow's peak. He was wearing dirty jeans and a denim jacket with the sleeves ripped off at the shoulder seams, and even in the dim light under the lowering clouds Rhodes could see the Los Muertos gang tattoo on his arm. He looked a little like Eddie Munster, grown old and gone to seed.

"Hey, Sheriff," Rapper said. "Fancy meeting you here."

"I didn't think I'd ever be seeing you again, Rapper. You must like it in Blacklin County."

Rapper held up a hand that was missing the ends of a couple of fingers, thanks to his last encounter with Rhodes.

"Not much," he said. "You know, I think if you'd cared about me, you'd have looked for the rest of my fingers. Maybe I could've had them reattached. They can do stuff like that now, even in backwoods towns like yours. These stumps hurt like hell when it rains like this."

Rhodes wasn't sympathetic. "Then you should stay out of the rain. In fact, maybe you should just stay out of the county. Why don't you pack your tent and move on before it gets completely dark. That way we won't have a problem."

Rapper turned to the tent next to his own. "You

hear that, Nellie? The sheriff thinks we oughta move on. What do you think?''

Nellie came out of the tent. He was pretty much as Rhodes remembered him, thinner and more fit-looking than Rapper, with wavy graying hair slicked back on the sides.

''You tryin' to tell us what to do, Sheriff?'' he asked. ''Seems like you'd have figured out by now that Rapper and I don't take very well to bein' told things. Ain't that right, Rapper?''

Rapper took a step toward Nellie and thumped him in the chest. ''I'll speak for myself, Nellie. When I ask you what you think, don't you ever try to speak for me.''

''Sorry, Rapper,'' Nellie said, cringing a little. ''I didn't mean anything by it.''

''And it won't happen again,'' Rapper said.

''And it won't happen again.'' Nellie backed up a step. ''I promise.''

''I guess I can't blame you for what you said, Sheriff,'' Rapper said, turning back to Rhodes. ''I guess it's just natural for you to get a little uppity with me, when even the help doesn't seem to know its place.''

''I'm not getting uppity,'' Rhodes said. ''I'm telling you to move on out of here.''

''I heard you, but we're not moving anywhere. We like it here.''

''Yeah,'' Nellie said. ''We like it here.''

Rapper didn't chastise him this time. Apparently it was all right for him to back up the boss, just as long as he didn't try to express the boss's thoughts.

"While you're here, then, we might as well have a little talk," Rhodes said.

"What about?" Rapper asked.

"About where you were last night around midnight."

"Why, that's pretty hard to remember," Rapper said. "Can you remember where we were, Nellie?"

"Not me. I was too drunk."

Rhodes looked at the two men. In the mist and the dark, standing in front of their tents, they looked like a couple of Neanderthals. All they needed was stone axes and a club.

Rapper stared back at Rhodes unconcernedly. He reached under his jacket and brought out a red and white crushproof box of cigarettes. Marlboros, Rhodes noticed as Rapper stuck one in the center of his tight little mouth and lit it with a green plastic lighter.

"It's too bad that you can't remember," Rhodes said. "I'll have to take you in for questioning, then."

"What's the charge?" Rapper asked.

"Trespassing."

"You must be getting forgetful in your old age, Sheriff," Rapper said, smoke curling around his head. "You know this land belongs to Nellie's uncle, and Nellie's uncle said it'd be just fine for us to stay here for as long as we wanted to."

"Even considering what happened the last time you were here?" Rhodes asked.

"We talked to him real polite," Rapper said. "We told him we'd clean up after ourselves and that we wouldn't piss in his lake."

"So what're you gonna do now, Sheriff?" Nellie asked. "Go away and leave us alone?"

"No, I'm not going to do that. I'm going to take you in."

"You got no grounds," Rapper said.

"Sure I have. Suspicion of murder."

"You must be crazy," Rapper said. He threw his cigarette to the ground and stepped on it. "We didn't kill anybody. You take us in and we'll be out in ten minutes."

"Maybe," Rhodes said. "Maybe not."

Rapper dragged a hand across his face to wipe away some of the water that had gathered there. He was still smiling.

"You're gonna need some help if you try that, Sheriff."

"And I don't see anybody else around here but you," Nellie said. "And us. Not unless they're hidin' in that county car. You got anybody in the trunk?"

Rhodes wondered where Ruth was. She should have been there by now. Then he remembered that he'd told Hack not to send her if she was busy. Maybe she'd been working on something.

But that wouldn't necessarily have mattered. Hack would have sent her anyway. He never listened to Rhodes.

If he'd sent her, though, where was she? Rhodes was beginning to regret having come out to the lake on his own. He was getting too old for this sort of thing. He reached for his sidearm, and as soon as he did, Nellie lunged for him, dropping his head low and bellowing like a bull.

Rhodes might have gotten the pistol out had he not taken a step backward in his surprise at Nellie's charge. His foot slipped in the mud, and he was halfway to the ground when Nellie hit him chest high, driving him further backward.

They hit the ground and skidded several feet in the muck. Nellie had his arms wrapped around Rhodes and was butting him in the chin with the top of his head. Rhodes gave up on trying to draw the pistol and concentrated on trying to break Nellie's hold before Rapper got to them and did something Rhodes would regret.

Just as he was thinking this, Nellie did something that Rhodes regretted—he broke the reading glasses in Rhodes's shirt pocket. Rhodes felt rather than heard the crack of the plastic frames.

For some reason that made Rhodes really angry. It was bad enough that he was rolling around in the mud with a cheap thug on top of him, but now his glasses were broken.

Not only that, he could hear the roar of a motorcycle being started.

He brought up a knee and slammed it hard into Nellie's scrotum. Nellie let out a high-pitched scream and let Rhodes go, rolling to the side and clutching himself while assuming the fetal position.

Rhodes drew his pistol, but it was too late to do anything with it unless he wanted to shoot Rapper in the back as he rode away.

He was so upset that he actually considered it for about half a second. Then he put the pistol back in its holster and went over to where Nellie was squirming on the ground.

"Looks like your buddy ran out on you," he said.

Nellie said something that sounded like, "Arrrgggghhhh."

"My sentiments exactly," Rhodes told him as he reached down to grab him by the shirt front.

Nellie tried to wriggle away, but Rhodes dragged him over to the county car and opened the back door. Nellie made a half-hearted attempt to bite the sheriff's wrist, but he was still in too much pain to do more than try. Rhodes flipped him over and grabbed his collar and belt.

"Watch your head," he said, and threw Nellie into the back seat.

Rhodes slammed the back door, securing Nellie in the car. The rain had stopped completely now, but the day was still dark and gloomy. Rhodes was cold, and he had mud all over his clothes and in his hair. He reached in his pocket and took out the glasses, which were in two pieces.

He supposed that he could tape them together with duct tape. Maybe nobody would notice. Or use Super Glue. That might work. Of course he could always buy a new pair at the drugstore. He tried to remember the strength that he used—2.5?

He put the glasses back in his pocket and went to look for the Marlboro butt. He found it crushed into the mud and picked it up. He could send it, along with the butt he'd found in the ashtray of Meredith's car, to the lab and have it tested. Saliva had plenty of DNA in it, and the lab should be able to tell him whether the same person had smoked both cigarettes.

He walked back to the car. The first thing he did after cranking the engine and turning on the heater was to call Hack and tell him to put out an all points bulletin for Rapper.

"What kinda motorsickle is he ridin'?" Hack wanted to know.

"I'm not sure," Rhodes said. "Nellie?"

There was no answer.

"Can you hear me, Nellie?"

This time there was a low groan from the back seat, but that was all.

"We'll have to find that out later. Or you can check your computer. What happened to Ruth, by the way?"

"She ain't there with you?"

Rhodes said that she wasn't.

"Well, I sent her along right after you came by the jail. I hope she's not in trouble."

Rhodes said that he hoped so too and signed off.

Turning to the back seat, he said, "Can you hear me, Nellie?"

Nellie groaned again.

"Good. I'm arresting you for assault of a police officer." Rhodes thought about his glasses and added, "And destruction of private property. Do you understand that?"

In a strained voice Nellie said, "You son of a bitch."

"And for abusive language. Now let me give you your rights."

Rhodes recited the Miranda rights. "Do you understand?" he asked.

Nellie didn't say a word.

"Exercising your right to remain silent. I don't blame you."

Rhodes was feeling a little better now. The warm air from the heater was taking a little of the chill away from his wet clothing. He backed the car up and headed it toward the rutted road.

"You'd better hope we don't get stuck," he told Nellie. "If we do, guess who'll have to get out and push?"

They didn't get stuck, however, and they got off the Gottschalk land and onto the county road without incident. They hadn't gone far toward Milsby before Rhodes saw Ruth Grady slogging toward him on foot. She looked dejected. Rhodes didn't blame her.

Knowing that it would be better not to stop, Rhodes stopped anyway on what he hoped was a relatively solid part of the road. He lowered his window and waited.

Ruth walked to where he was parked and looked in the window. "I guess I wasn't much help," she said.

"No problem," Rhodes said. He nodded toward the back seat. "You remember our friend Nellie?"

"How could I forget? Is he the one who got you so muddy?"

"Broke my glasses, too," Rhodes said. "Get in and we'll deliver him to the jail."

"What about my car?"

"Where is it?"

"In the ditch. We'll pass it right around the next bend. I guess I got in too much of a hurry. It started sliding on the mud, and before I knew it, I was off the road and in the ditch."

"I'll call Hack. He'll send Henry out for it."

Henry Jenkins was the owner of Henry's Full Service Station, the only place in Clearview where you could still buy gas and get it pumped by someone other than yourself. Henry would wash your windshield and check your tires, too. He also ran a wrecker service.

Ruth walked around the car and got in. "I could have called Hack myself. I just hated to do it."

Rhodes could understand why. When Ruth had come to work for the county, Hack hadn't been very receptive to the idea of a female deputy. Ruth had won him over quickly, however, and she obviously didn't want to disappoint him.

"We'll tell him a cow ran in front of you," Rhodes said.

Ruth laughed. "Let's just tell him the truth. I just hope he doesn't make any jokes about women drivers."

Rhodes called in, and Hack was sympathetic rather than accusing.

"Those roads oughta be paved," he said. "Or at least have a good gravel toppin' put on 'em. Why don't you talk to the commissioners about that? There's always somebody runnin' off in a ditch when it rains."

"I'm not sure the commissioners want to talk about the roads right now," Rhodes said. "They're more interested in finding out about Brady Meredith.''

"I guess so," Hack said. "I'll call Henry and have him bring the car in unless Ruth's gonna wait there and drive it."

"I'll bring Ruth," Rhodes told him. "I have some things to go over with her."

"Roger," Hack said. "Over and out."

Rhodes wondered if the dispatcher had been watching a rerun of "Highway Patrol."

"What do we have to talk over?" Ruth asked.

"Brady Meredith. I'm going to give you a few leads to check out."

"Good. I'll try not to get stuck in a ditch while I'm doing it."

"Forget about that. If I had a dime for every time I've been stuck, I'd be a rich man."

"All right. What do you want me to do?"

Rhodes told her.

EIGHT

AFTER A LONG HOT SHOWER, Rhodes felt much better. Ivy would be home from work in a few minutes, and maybe he could talk her into going to the Jolly Tamale for supper. He could use something decadent, like a chile relleno.

While he was waiting for Ivy, he went out to feed Speedo, whose real name was Mr. Earl. The dog bounded up to the door when Rhodes rattled the food bag, and Rhodes filled the dog bowl with Ol' Roy.

Speedo had recently come up in the world, thanks to a friend of Ivy's who had built him a real dog house. It was made of wood and insulated with Styrofoam, quite a change from the barrel full of hay that Rhodes had provided for him. Rhodes hoped Speedo appreciated his new digs, but it was hard to tell. Speedo spent most of his time roaming around the yard, and he seemed to prefer to sleep under the big pecan tree in the corner.

Ivy drove up just as Speedo was polishing the bottom of the food bowl, and the dog ran over to greet her, jumping up on the side of the car and looking in through the window.

"It's just Ivy," Rhodes told him. "Don't get so excited."

"I heard that," Ivy said, getting out of the car.

She patted Speedo on the head. "Has the magic gone out of our marriage so soon?"

"I didn't mean that the way it sounded," Rhodes said, wondering if he was just making things worse.

"You silver-tongued devil," Ivy said. She kissed him on the cheek. "And clean, too. Have you been washing off some hussy's perfume?"

"I had a long day," Rhodes said.

There was still some dampness in the air, but the clouds were beginning to break up. In the west they were rimmed with the red of the sunset.

"I know," Ivy said. "I heard about Brady Meredith."

"Did you hear that Rapper's back?"

Ivy hadn't heard that, and Rhodes told her about his tussle with Nellie.

"Why don't we go to the Jolly Tamale tonight," Ivy said when he'd finished. "I'm in the mood for some chicken fajitas."

"If that's what you want, I'll go," Rhodes said. "That stuff has a lot of fat grams in it, though."

Ivy poked a finger in his stomach. "You could stand a few fat grams. Don't be such a fanatic."

"Well, if you insist," Rhodes said.

THEY STOPPED AT the drugstore on the way so Rhodes could buy a new pair of glasses. He was afraid that he wouldn't be able to read the menu without them.

Not long afterward, he was at the Jolly Tamale, looking at a battered and deep-fried poblano pepper stuffed with jack cheese and covered with ranchero sauce. He thought he could feel his arteries clogging before he even stuck his fork in it.

"So what are you going to do?" Ivy asked as she squeezed a quarter of a lemon over her sizzling fajitas. "Everyone at work has already asked me if you'd have things taken care of before the bi-district game."

They were sitting side by side in a corner booth and there wasn't much likelihood of anyone's overhearing them. The Jolly Tamale was a noisy family place, and everyone else was absorbed in loud conversation. It had to be loud to carry over the crying of the two babies who were shrieking at widely separated tables, the jangle of silverware, and the clatter of dishes from the kitchen. But since Ivy and Rhodes were sitting so close to each other, they could converse in normal tones.

While they were waiting for their order, Rhodes had told Ivy about what he'd been doing besides rolling in the mud with Nellie. There was too much still to be done for him to take care of all of it.

"I've split things up with Ruth Grady," he said. "She's going to talk to Bob Deedham and his wife tonight. Deedham really seemed to dislike Meredith, and he tried to throw suspicion off on Jasper Knowles. Maybe Ruth can find out what's going on there."

"Jealousy is a powerful motive," Ivy said. "I've seen his wife. She's very attractive."

"Maybe that's it," Rhodes said, cutting into the chile relleno with his fork. Steam rose into the air.

"And where will you be going tonight?" Ivy asked.

Rhodes had figured that question was coming, but Ivy had gradually gotten used to his not being at home in the evenings when he was working on a case. She still didn't like it, but she didn't complain. She knew it was part of the job, and that the job was important to him.

Rhodes tried a bite of the chile. It was still too hot to eat.

"First I'm going to talk to Jasper Knowles. Then I'm going to The County Line and see if I can find out what Rapper's been up to out there, or if he's been there at all. And to find out if Brady Meredith has really been going there to drink."

"What about Hayes Ford?"

"I'll talk to him tomorrow. Sunday morning is probably the best time of the week to catch him at home. And tomorrow afternoon I'll talk to the players before they watch the game films. That is, if the film study is still going on as planned. I'll ask Jasper about that."

"When's the funeral?"

"I don't know. I have to talk to Nancy Meredith again, anyway. I'll ask her."

"I suppose that about covers it," Ivy said. "I probably won't be seeing a lot of you for the rest of the weekend, will I?"

"Probably not," Rhodes said.

He had a nagging feeling that what Ivy had said about his having things covered wasn't exactly true, that there was something that he was overlooking, but he couldn't think of what it might be.

He tried the chile relleno again. This time it was just right.

JASPER KNOWLES SAT on his black leather couch with his wife, Velma, beside him. In her youth, she had played basketball with the Wayland Baptist College Flying Queens, and she was almost as big as Jasper, with once-blonde hair now going gray in front and a sizable gap between her top front teeth.

She didn't like it at all that Rhodes was there to talk to her husband.

"I hope you don't consider Jasper a suspect," she said. "There's no way he could have been involved in anything like that."

"I just want to clarify a few things," Rhodes said. "Jasper's not a suspect."

That wasn't really true. At this point, everyone was a suspect, but there was no need to tell Velma Knowles that. She wouldn't understand.

"You don't have to worry about the sheriff," Jasper said. "He knows me. He knows that I wouldn't kill anyone. Go ahead and ask your questions, Sheriff."

Rhodes was sitting across from the Knowleses in a leather recliner. He kept sliding toward the back, so he tried to sit on the front edge of the seat and lean forward.

"It's about something that Bob Deedham mentioned today," he said. "He said that you and Brady Meredith hadn't gotten along all year."

"Brady was a troublemaker," Velma Knowles

said. "He thought *he* was the head coach. He didn't know how to follow orders."

Jasper patted his wife's knee. "I can speak for myself, Vel."

Rhodes was glad to see that Jasper wasn't quite as emphatic as Rapper had been in expressing more or less the same idea to Nellie.

"Well," Velma said, "I hope you'll tell the sheriff about how Brady wouldn't do what you told him to and how he called plays that you didn't authorize."

"Brady was in charge of the offense," Jasper pointed out. "He was supposed to call the plays."

"Not some of the plays he called, he wasn't. You told me so yourself."

Jasper looked at Rhodes and shrugged. "She's right. The coaches work out an offensive and defensive game plan every week, and Brady and I went over the offensive plays. We were supposed to more or less agree about what he'd call in certain situations, but he didn't always follow the plan."

"Like last night?" Rhodes asked.

"Well, not exactly. We'd never been in that situation before. Most of our games weren't that close."

He and Rhodes smiled at that. None of the Clearview games had been remotely that close.

"Give me a couple of examples," Rhodes said.

"Tell him about the Westico game," Velma said. "Tell him about that one."

The Westico game had been out of town, so Rhodes hadn't seen it. He went only to the ones played locally.

"What happened?" he asked.

"Lord knows, that one was strange," Jasper said. "Brady called for a punt on a third down, when we were on the forty-yard line."

"*Their* forty-yard line," Velma pointed out. "And we were moving the ball on every play. I thought I was going to have a stroke right there in the stands when I saw the kicker run out on the field."

"Well, we were a long way ahead," Jasper said. "Maybe Brady was tryin' to keep the score down."

Rhodes wondered if Brady might have been trying to do a little point shaving. He was beginning to think that maybe he should go ahead and try to talk to Hayes Ford tonight, but of course there was no use in that. Ford would be off somewhere in a card game, probably in another county, and there would be no finding him.

"Was there anything else like that?" Rhodes asked. "When the team was moving the ball and Brady put a stop to it?"

"Sounds pretty funny when you put it like that," Jasper said.

"I'm not laughing," Velma told him.

"Funny strange, Vel, not funny ha-ha," Jasper said. "And there was another time, all right."

"It was the Fondrell game," Velma said. "Brady called three straight passes into the end zone, every one of them to D'Andre Jackson, and he couldn't catch a ball if it had handles all over it."

"He's our blocking tight end," Jasper explained. "We put him in on the goal line when we're going to run the ball, but this time we didn't run it."

"Did you have words with Brady about the Westico game or the one with Fondrell?" Rhodes asked.

"You bet he did," Velma said. "You would too if you were the head coach. Brady was a little too big for his britches if you ask me."

Nobody had asked her, and it suddenly seemed to dawn on her that maybe she had talked a bit too much.

"Not that what he did would be any reason to kill him," she said. "He just needed a good talking to, and that's what Jasper gave him. A good talking to. Isn't that right, Jasper?"

"That's right," Jasper agreed.

"Where?" Rhodes asked. "On the sidelines or in the dressing room?"

"I waited until after the game, of course. It's not good for the team to see the coaches arguing. I thought Brady knew that, too, until last night."

"But Deedham knew about the arguments," Rhodes said.

"He might have overheard me talking to Brady. It was after the team had dressed and left. We were in my office, and I didn't exactly keep my voice down."

"Did Brady have any excuses for what he did?"

"He told me he was trying to fool the Fondrell defense," Jasper said. "He said we always ran when D'Andre was in the game, so he thought he'd cross 'em up and try a pass."

"That D'Andre couldn't catch a cold," Velma said. "He's a good blocker, though."

"What about the Westico game?" Rhodes asked.

"He said he lost track of the downs," Jasper said.

"And last night he lost track of the penetrations," Velma said. "You'd think a college graduate could count higher than five, wouldn't you?"

She didn't seem to expect an answer, so Rhodes didn't offer one.

"Will you be showing the game films tomorrow?" he asked Jasper.

"I guess so. The funeral's not until Monday. We'll have a team meeting, and then look at the films."

"How's Meredith's wife taking it?"

"Better than you'd think," Velma said. "I was over there this afternoon, and she cried a little. Then she washed her face and she was fine. I went over to Ballinger's with her to pick out the casket. She got a real nice one."

Rhodes couldn't think of anything more to ask. He didn't find much useful in Brady's disagreements with Knowles. All coaches had their differences.

"I appreciate your help," Rhodes said. "I'd like to meet with the team tomorrow, before you show the game films, if that's all right."

Knowles nodded. "Come by the field house about two o'clock. You can talk to the boys then."

Rhodes stood up. "By the way, do you know whether anybody on the team is using steroids?"

"You should be ashamed of yourself!" Velma said. "I can't believe you'd ask Jasper any such question. He runs a clean program, and he always has. Not a one of those boys would dream of taking a drug like that. Why, it can do all kinds of terrible things to you!"

"Good Lord, don't get all worked up, Vel," Jasper said. "Sheriff, I don't know what you've heard, but Vel's right. Those boys don't use any drugs. I don't even let 'em get B-twelve shots unless they're under doctor's orders."

"They seemed a little contentious last night. I know that's one of the side effects."

"So's bad skin," Velma said. "I hope you're not going out and try to arrest every boy in Clearview with pimples. You wouldn't have enough room in the jail to hold them."

Rhodes figured she was right about that. Maybe there was no basis for the rumor. But then there was Rapper.

"You're right," he said. "We'd have to build a new wing, and the commissioners wouldn't stand for that. It was just a stray rumor. I had to ask about it."

"Sure you did," Jasper said. "I understand."

He appeared to, Rhodes thought, but Velma didn't. If looks could kill, Ivy would be the next widow picking out a casket. He hoped she'd get him a real nice one.

"What other rumors have you heard?" Velma asked.

"None," Rhodes said. "But I saw someone that looked a little like Brady last night right before the game started. He was outside the stadium talking to Hayes Ford."

"My God," Velma said. "The biggest gambler in the county, and you think Brady was in with him. First the steroids, and now this! Next you're going to accuse us of shooting JFK!"

"Brady did go somewhere before the kickoff," Jasper said, trying to ignore his wife. "I thought he had to go take a pee."

"Jasper!" Velma said.

"Well, I did, Vel. Surely he wouldn't be crazy enough to talk to Ford right before a game." He stopped and thought a second. "But that might explain those funny calls he made for the offense. You think he was gambling, Sheriff?"

"I don't know," Rhodes said. "But I'm going to try to find out."

NINE

MOST PEOPLE WHO operated dancing and drinking establishments these days preferred to call their places "clubs," no matter what they looked like. But The County Line was a honky-tonk. There was no other word for it.

It was located seventeen miles to the southeast of Clearview, a low, sprawling building that sat about thirty yards off the road. The parking lot was white gravel with no lines and no rules. You parked where you could find a spot. Those who arrived early had to be very choosy about where they left their cars, or they might find that there was no way out until the parking lot cleared.

There were lights strung in the limbs of the live oaks and pecan trees growing next to and in back of the building, with tables underneath. There was even a wooden dance floor in back with a speaker from the jukebox dangling from a tree limb overhead. When the weather was good, couples could sit at the tables and enjoy the fresh air, though Rhodes didn't think that most of The County Line's customers were really the fresh-air type. There were no windows in the building at all.

He could hear the jukebox when he stepped out of his car. Someone Rhodes didn't recognize was singing. He knew it would be somebody who wore a big white hat, which seemed to be what all the singers wore these days—at least the ones who weren't wearing big black hats. The singers were as hard to tell apart as their songs.

Rhodes felt a brief tug of nostalgia for the days when you could hear Merle Haggard on the radio. No self-respecting country station would play Merle today, and no one would put him on a jukebox, either, which is why Rhodes had just about stopped listening to country radio. He'd never been much for jukeboxes.

He started across the parking lot, threading his way through the tangle of vehicles. The majority of them were pickups, some old, some battered, and some shiny new; but there were also quite a few cars, and even a couple of semi tractors. Near the building stood five motorcycles.

The County Line didn't put up much of a front. The white paint was old and cracking, and there was no lighted sign to let a casual passerby know the place's name. THE COUNTY LINE was printed over the double doorway in peeling black paint.

Rhodes opened the doors and went inside. The front room was a combination bar-restaurant with no pretensions. If you wanted a drink, you could have a beer. If you wanted to eat, you could get a hamburger, a cheeseburger, or a chicken-fried steak. There were only five booths. Eating wasn't the first thing on the minds of most of the visitors to The County Line.

Beyond the front room was the dance floor, which took up all the rest of the available space, not counting the seating area that ran along two sides and a small stage at the far end, which was reserved for the live band that would go on later in the evening.

There was a chicken-wire barricade in front of the stage so the band members wouldn't be injured if a fight erupted. Or if the dancers and listeners decided to show their disapproval of the band's selections or playing skill by throwing the nearest thing at hand— a beer bottle, a chair, or a friend. You didn't get the cream of Blacklin County society in The County Line.

The music was much louder inside the building than Rhodes had expected it to be when he entered the parking lot. He was pretty sure he could feel the floor pulsating under his feet. He stood in the doorway for a minute to let his ears adjust to the noise and his eyes to the dim light, most of which seemed to come from an array of neon beer signs behind the bar. The signs advertised every brand of beer that Rhodes had ever heard of, including Hamm's, "the beer refreshing," which he wasn't sure was even being brewed any longer. Even if it was, he didn't think you could buy it in Texas.

There were no "no smoking" sections in The County Line. A filmy haze hung just below the ceiling, and the smoke tickled Rhodes's nose and throat. He resisted the urge to sneeze.

Most of the people Rhodes could see were dressed in full honky-tonk drag. The men wore tight Levi's or Wrangler jeans, wide hand-tooled belts with names like Buddy and Joe Don inscribed on the buckles, Western shirts, and cowboy boots.

As for the women, Rhodes guessed that there was enough hair in The County Line to stuff about seven hundred mattresses. How much of it was actually growing on the heads it seemed to sprout from, and how much of it was part of elaborate wigs, he couldn't even begin to guess. Big hair was a longtime Texas tradition, but there were women here who couldn't walk under a ceiling fan without risking catastrophe. And it seemed to Rhodes that there weren't any moderate shadings to the hair. It was all very blonde, very red, or very black.

And if the jeans on the men were tight, there'd have to be a new word invented to describe the way the women's fit. Most of the women looked as they'd lain down on their beds to wiggle into their pants, then gotten into a tub of hot water and let the jeans shrink even more.

Not everyone was dressed that way, of course. There were a couple of bikers at the bar, dressed pretty much the way Rapper had been, except that one of them was wearing a leather jacket and the other had on a T-shirt that said BORN TOO LOOSE in red letters. He either had a sense of humor or he couldn't spell. Rhodes didn't figure it made any difference.

Rhodes walked over to the bar, standing at the end away from the bikers. He had Rapper's old mug shot and a newspaper photo of Brady Meredith in his pocket, and he took them out while he waited for the bartender to come over. Under the beer signs in front of Rhodes there was a fake-rustic wooden sign that said, EVEN A FISH WOULDN'T GET CAUGHT IF HE KEPT

HIS MOUTH SHUT. Rhodes hoped the bartender didn't take the sign seriously.

The bartender took his time. He gave a couple of bottles of beer to the bikers, wiped the bar with a cloth that looked none too clean, and then wandered down to the sheriff.

"Well?" he said.

Rhodes had dealt with him once or twice before, when fights in the parking lot had gotten so far out of hand that someone actually called for the law. He was taller than Rhodes and quite fat. In fact, standing across the bar from him, Rhodes felt almost slim. The bartender had a surprisingly high voice for a man so huge, but it cut through the noise of the music easily.

"Well?" he said again.

Rhodes laid the pictures of Rapper and Meredith on the bar next to a bowl of peanuts. "When's the last time either of these two was in here?"

The bartender hardly glanced down. "Never saw 'em before."

Rhodes shook his head. "Now, Zach. You know better than that."

Zack looked out over the crowd on the dance floor. "I don't want to get mixed up in any murder, Sheriff."

"I'm not asking you about a murder. I just want to know when you saw these two men."

"That one's dead," Zack said, putting a fat, damp finger on Meredith's face. "The coach. I heard all about it."

"What about the other one?"

Zach gave a sidelong glance down the bar at the two bikers, who were both now looking at Rhodes.

"They don't like you much," Zach said.

"I probably wouldn't like them if I got to know them. They have any connection with this guy?"

"I don't know anything about that. He's been in once, last weekend."

"Did he talk to Meredith?"

"Not that I know of. The coach was more interested in better-looking conversationalists, if you know what I mean."

"I think I can figure it out. Do you have any names for me?"

"I don't ask names. I just hand out beers. You want one, by the way?"

"No thanks. You have any Dr. Pepper?"

Zach didn't bother to answer that one.

"She was a looker, though," he said after a pause. "The one the coach talked to. Blonde, and built."

That description, sketchy as it was, pretty well matched the one that Goober Vance had given Rhodes of Bob Deedham's wife, but then, about half the women in The County Line matched that description.

"Can you be a little more specific?" Rhodes asked.

Zach shook his head slightly. "Nope."

"What did he have to drink? The coach, I mean."

"He never had more than a couple of beers. I don't know why he didn't just buy him some at the grocery store and drink 'em at home."

"Maybe he couldn't get the same kind of conversation at home," Rhodes said.

"I know what you mean," Zach said, looking out at the dance floor. "You can sure find it here, though, if you want it. I guess that's why the coaches like it here."

Rhodes had been about to ask something about Rapper, but he suddenly changed his mind.

"Coaches," he said. "More than one?"

"Did I say that? I musta been thinking of something else. I didn't mean anything by it."

"I think you did," Rhodes told him. "How many coaches have been coming in here, anyway?"

"Just the one," Zach said, looking over the top of Rhodes's head.

"Is that a roach I see on the floor over there?" Rhodes asked. "I think the county health inspector better come have a look at this place tomorrow. And every day after that, for about a month."

"That's blackmail," Zach said.

"Just genuine concern for the health of the voting public. They'll thank me for it later."

"All right, all right. I get it. There was another one of the coaches in here. The one that really looks like a football player, that Needham."

"Deedham," Rhodes said.

"That's the one. Played pro for a while."

"Not really," Rhodes said. "When was he here?"

Zach had to think about that. "Now that you mention it, he was here the last time that Meredith was, last Saturday night."

"Did they have a drink together?"

"I don't think they even saw each other. Meredith was in there dancing and talking to that blonde. Deedham was in here at the bar."

"Did he have much to drink?"

"Just one beer. Then he left."

"What kind of mood was he in?" Rhodes asked.

"Hey, I can't remember everything. He looked OK, I guess. I gotta go now. I got some customers."

Two men in jeans and a woman with hair so blonde that it was nearly white stood a little way down the bar. The woman was laughing at something one of the men had said.

As Zach moved away, Rhodes said, "Come back when you're through with them."

While Zach was gone, Rhodes thought about what the bartender had told him. Could it be that Deedham had followed his wife to The County Line and seen her with Meredith? If he had, could that have led to Meredith's murder? And where did Rapper fit into all this?

The jukebox played two indistinguishable songs before Zach returned.

"Band's gonna come on in about half an hour," Zach said. "Tommy and the Texans. You ever hear 'em?"

"Does Tommy wear a big white hat?"

"That's him."

"Then I've heard him. Or somebody just like him." Rhodes tapped Rapper's photo. "Now about this one."

"Nothin' to tell about that one. He comes in, he leaves. We get bikers here now and then." Zach looked back down the bar, but the two bikers had left. "They usually don't stay long, though."

"When was he here?"

"Don't remember. But it wasn't long ago. Last week sometime, I guess."

"Think about it."

Zach thought. It didn't do any good. "He didn't do anything, just had a beer or two and left, like those guys did." He motioned to where the bikers had been. "I just serve the beer. I don't keep up with 'em."

"All right, Zach. I appreciate the conversation."

"Well, I don't. Nothing against you personally, Sheriff, but I'd just as soon not have you comin' in here. It's not all that good for business."

"I'll keep that in mind," Rhodes said.

A THIN SLIVER OF MOON hung in a clearing between two cloud banks, and a few stars twinkled in the black sky. Rhodes took a breath of the rain-washed air, a real pleasure after the smoke-filled building. He'd have to throw his clothes in the hamper when he got home.

As he moved to his left to avoid a puddle, the two bikers who had been at the bar stepped around a Ford Ranger and stood in front of him. They seemed bigger than they had when they'd been fifteen feet away.

The one in the leather jacket smiled broadly, revealing an amazingly white and even set of teeth, which Rhodes realized must be false. Rhodes didn't even want to think about how he might have lost the originals.

"Evenin', Sheriff," he said.

"Evenin'," Rhodes answered. "Do I know you?"

"I don't think so. But you know a friend of ours."

"Rapper?"

"That's the one. You shouldn't be hasslin' him, Sheriff. He's a good ol' boy, wouldn't hurt a fly."

Rhodes had to smile at that. It was about as far from describing Rapper as you could get.

"Have you seen him tonight?" he asked.

The one in the T-shirt didn't smile. He didn't look as if he knew how.

He said, "Nope, we ain't seen him tonight. And we won't see him, either. You scared him so bad, he's left the county."

Rhodes smiled again. If these two got any funnier, they could get their own sitcom.

"I didn't know he scared so easily. And I'm surprised he'd run off and leave his buddy in jail."

"Don't you worry about Nellie. He'll be out in the mornin', soon as he pays his fine."

"I wasn't worrying about him. I'm going to have to ask him a few questions before he leaves, though. And I'd like to talk to Rapper again."

"Look, Sheriff," the one with the teeth said, "all we want is to be left alone. We didn't come here to make any trouble for you, and we'll be leavin' quietly."

Rhodes didn't believe a word of it. *Quietly* wasn't in a biker's vocabulary.

"You tell Rapper I want to talk to him," Rhodes said. "Tell him that I don't think it would be a good idea for him to leave the county without coming by to see me. I'd have to see to it that he was arrested and brought back.''

The two men glanced at each other, then looked back at Rhodes. T-shirt took a step closer to the sheriff. He was close enough to touch now, if Rhodes had wanted to touch him—which, of course, he didn't, because he could also smell him. He smelled as if he hadn't had a bath in quite a while. Within, say, the last couple of years.

''People don't tell Rapper what to do and what not to do,'' T-shirt said.

''I do,'' Rhodes said. ''Maybe you're forgetting that I'm the sheriff.''

''We're not forgettin'. We're just wonderin' how come you think you can talk so big without any deputies to back you up.''

Rhodes hadn't thought he'd need any backup at The County Line. He hadn't counted on any trouble.

''I don't need any deputies. If you two make trouble, I'll have to take you in. Ask Rapper. Or ask Nellie. They can tell you.''

T-shirt had apparently already spoken to Rapper, or, if not, he seemed to know that Rhodes meant what he said. He stepped back.

''We ain't gonna cause any trouble. We're just tellin' you to lay off Rapper. He's not mixed up in any murder. And you could be sorry if you keep on hasslin' him.''

''Maybe Nellie can tell me what I want to know,'' Rhodes said. ''Since I already have him, I'll ask him. That way, Rapper won't be bothered so much.''

"Nellie won't tell you a thing. That's not the way Nellie operates."

"Maybe not, but it won't hurt to try."

Rhodes was tired of the conversation. It wasn't going anywhere. He walked between the two men, brushing his shoulder against the leather jacket. The man stepped aside, putting his foot into a puddle of rainwater.

"Son of a *bitch!*" he said.

Rhodes stopped and turned around. The two men looked at him; Rhodes looked back. After a few seconds, they dropped their eyes.

Leather Jacket looked down at his foot. He was wearing a heavy motorcycle boot, made darker by the water that had soaked into it.

"That water's *cold,*" he said. He shook his foot as if hoping to dry it.

Rhodes said. "Better go put on some dry socks. You could catch a cold if you don't take care of yourself, and dry that boot at room temperature. That way the leather won't crack." He turned to walk away. "You fellas drive carefully now."

"You're the one that better be careful," T-shirt called after him. "You never know what kind of mess you might get into."

Rhodes didn't bother to turn around and answer him, but the truth was that Rhodes had a pretty good idea. He'd been in too many messes before.

TEN

It was not quite nine o'clock, so Rhodes thought it wouldn't be too late to drive by and have his talk with Nancy Meredith. Maybe she would be a little more forthcoming than Rapper's two friends.

There were several cars parked in front of the Meredith house when he got there. The relatives had begun to arrive. Rhodes was met at the door by Nancy's mother, a short, birdlike woman who told him that her daughter was too distraught to talk to him.

Rhodes was about to leave when Nancy came up behind her mother and said, "If it's about Brady, I can talk to him. Maybe he knows who did it."

Rhodes said that he didn't know, but that she might be able to help him if she answered a few questions.

"We can talk in the TV room, then," Nancy said, ignoring her mother's obvious disapproval. "Everybody else is in the kitchen."

The TV room was a small bedroom that had been converted into an entertainment area. There was a couch against one wall, and a television set with a twenty-seven-inch screen sat against the opposite wall. The only other furniture in the room was a small end table by the arm of the couch. A copy of the latest *Reader's Digest* lay on the table.

Nancy Meredith sat on the couch, and since there wasn't any other choice, Rhodes sat beside her. He looked around and saw her mother hovering in the doorway.

"It's all right, Mother," Nancy said. "I'll be fine. You go on in with the others. I'll be there when we're done."

Her mother stood indecisively for a few seconds and then turned and walked away without a word.

"Now, then," Nancy said. "What did you want to ask me, Sheriff?"

"In cases like this we have to deal with some pretty delicate matters," Rhodes said. "I hope you won't think I'm trying to discredit your husband's memory by anything I have to say."

"You're talking about that Deedham bitch, aren't you."

Rhodes was a little shocked at her choice of words. He was a little old-fashioned, and it seemed strange to him to hear a coach's wife use language like that.

"Uh, maybe," he said.

"Oh, don't be so embarrassed," Nancy said. "I knew about her, all right. She'd been after Brady for more than a year. He'd sneak off to that honky tonk, thinking I didn't know that she'd be there. He should have known you can't fool a wife about those things."

"Who told you she'd be there?"

"Nobody had to tell me. I could see the way she'd look at him when she didn't think Bob and I were watching. She had to meet him somewhere."

"Bob knew, too?"

"Of course he did. Brady wasn't the first one she'd made a run at."

"Who else?"

"Roy Kenner, for one. But his wife's like me. She knew that Roy had better sense than to get hooked up with someone like Terry."

Rhodes was beginning to wish that he'd taken on the questioning of the Deedhams personally. Purely academic curiosity, he told himself. Nothing to do with getting a look at Terry.

"How did Bob take all this?"

"That's hard to say. He's really wrapped up in his job, you know? I think that's part of Terry's problem, really, and I'm sorry I called her a bitch, even if she is one. She probably doesn't have much of a home life. But Brady does." She caught herself. "Did, I mean. So does Roy Kenner. They didn't need her."

Rhodes thought that it might be a good idea to have a talk with Roy Kenner anyway.

"Brady needed to go to The County Line," he said, "Or he thought he did. Home life or not."

"There was nothing wrong with him going out there. I knew he went, and I didn't mind. He needed some way to blow off a little steam after a week of building up to the game. There's a lot of pressure on a coach, and it doesn't get any better when you start winning. He thought it was a good idea to go where there was a little music and some bright lights, and somewhere that was a long way from town so no one would see him and comment on it."

"What about the people who saw him there? There must have been a lot of them."

"They weren't in any position to criticize, you know? Anyway, he never drank much, and he never stayed out there very long."

She didn't seem upset at all by her husband's having had a few beers each weekend, though the fact that Terry Deedham had met him at the honky-tonk bothered her a little. Rhodes thought it might be a good idea to probe that some more.

"Did he ever dance with Terry? There's a lot of dancing at The County Line."

Nancy Meredith sat up a little straighter. "I never asked him. I knew she went out there, but I trusted Brady, and that was enough for me."

"How did you know about her going out there?"

"You hear things. She went all the time. I'll bet she was very popular with some people."

"And you don't know how Bob reacted to that?"

"He didn't like it, I'm sure. Would you, if it were your wife? But if you're wondering whether he was jealous enough to kill Brady, I'm sure I don't know. If he was, and if he did, I hope you put him so far back in that jail of yours that he never sees the light of day again."

The jail wasn't quite that big, but Rhodes didn't see any need to mention it.

"There are a couple of other things," he said.

Nancy looked down at her hands, which were clasped in her lap. She rubbed her thumbs together and said, "All right. Go ahead."

"It has to do with gambling," Rhodes said. "I saw someone that looked a lot like Brady talking to

Hayes Ford just before the game last night. Do you know who Hayes Ford is?''

"I know who he is, all right, and I can tell for sure Brady didn't gamble," Nancy said, but her voice weakened at the end, and Rhodes knew she was covering something up.

"Were you two in debt? Did you need money?"

Nancy looked away, and Rhodes said, "You might as well tell me. I can find out anyway."

Nancy stood up and walked over to the TV set. Then she turned to Rhodes.

"It's Brady's father," she said. "He's got Alzheimer's."

For her, that seemed to explain everything, but it wasn't enough for Rhodes. He asked her to go on.

"Do you know how much nursing homes charge? Nearly three thousand dollars a month, at least, and that doesn't count medicine."

Rhodes knew what she was getting at now.

"Brady's mother is still alive," he said.

"That's right. And that means she has to pay for his father's care until she's reduced to two thousand dollars in the bank. The government will help out then. Oh, and she gets to keep her house and her car. Isn't that nice?"

"So Brady was trying to help her?"

"He and his brother. It's quite a strain on our finances, even with both of us teaching. We've been sending some money, but Brady wouldn't talk about where he got it. I don't know what will happen to his mother now. I guess she'll lose everything."

"So Brady gambled to get money."

"I don't know that," Nancy Meredith said.

"But you suspect it."

"I'm not sure. Someone used to call here and ask for Brady. He'd never give his name, but I thought I heard Brady call him 'Ford' once."

Rhodes didn't know much about the University Interscholastic League's rules, but it seemed likely that Clearview would have to forfeit its games if it were proven that Brady had been gambling. Rhodes hated to think what that might mean to the town.

"What about money changing hands?"

"I don't know anything about that. I know Brady was sending money home, but we never had much in the bank, that's for sure."

Which didn't prove anything. Brady could have been using cash. Or, if he'd been winning, he could have been taking cash. That's the only way Hayes Ford worked, in fact. No need in letting the IRS get its hands on your hard-earned money if it could be avoided.

"There's still something else," Rhodes said.

Nancy seemed to grow even smaller.

"You're not joking, are you?" she asked. She looked at Rhodes and shook her head. "No, you wouldn't joke about something like that. What else, then?"

"I've heard a rumor that some of the players are taking steroids," he said.

Nancy giggled with relief. "That's one thing you don't have to worry about involving Brady in. He hated drugs. He didn't even like to take aspirin when he had a headache. He always said he didn't like the idea of letting some drug have more control over his body and mind than he did. He didn't even like for the boys to drink soda that has caffeine.''

Rhodes was beginning to wonder just how reliable a source Goober Vance was. Most of his suggestions were turning out to be nothing more than gossip, and gossip that didn't have much of a basis in fact.

If Nancy were telling the truth, and Rhodes believed that she was, Brady wasn't chasing Terry Deedham; she was chasing him. And unless Jasper Knowles, his wife, and Nancy were all lying, no one had heard the rumors about steroids.

But Rhodes still felt that Rapper was mixed up in things somehow, and to Rhodes that meant drugs of some kind or another. He wasn't going to give up that angle just yet.

"I notice that there aren't any ashtrays in the house," Rhodes said. "I suppose that with your husband's attitude toward drugs, he didn't smoke."

"He hated smoking," Nancy said. "That was the one thing he didn't like about The County Line. His clothes always smelled like smoke after he'd been there."

Rhodes knew what she meant. "And I guess he had strict rules for the players."

"He sure did. Smoking was one thing he and Jasper agreed on."

"They didn't always agree on what plays to call, did they?"

"Not always. They got into a few arguments about it, because Brady was a little bullheaded about calling what he thought was right. I guess that's what happened last night.''

Rhodes wasn't so sure about that. He was practically convinced that Brady had been involved in shaving points, or trying to. He didn't know how he was going to prove it, though.

"There's one thing I want you to know, Sheriff,'' Nancy said, breaking in on Rhodes's thoughts.

"What's that?''

"I loved Brady, and I want you to find out who killed him. I can accept that he's dead, but he was a good man, no matter what you've been thinking. He had a few drinks, but that was just one night a week. He didn't chase that Deedham woman, and he didn't let his players take steroids. He might have gambled, or he might not. I can't say for sure about that. I don't like to think that he did, but he might have. He needed money, all right. Anyway, none of that matters to me. What matters is that he was a good husband and I loved him. Somebody has to pay for killing him. I want you to promise me that you'll find out who it was and make sure they suffer for it.''

It was a promise that Rhodes would have liked to make, but he knew that he couldn't. He'd do what he could to find the killer. That was his job. Making the killer suffer wasn't. But he didn't have to tell Nancy Meredith that.

"I'll do what I can,'' he said, and that was the truth.

LAWTON AND HACK were waiting for Rhodes when he got to the jail. He knew that spelled trouble, but he didn't know what kind. He also knew that it wouldn't do any good to ask, but he did it anyway.

"Has there been anything going on tonight?"

Lawton cut a glance at Hack. Hack, being the dispatcher, claimed first right to tell all the stories, though Lawton often tried to jump in first. If he did, that just made things worse, and Rhodes hoped he'd keep his mouth shut.

But he didn't. He said, "Been a criminal assault."

Rhodes had been feeling tired, but he got a sudden jolt of adrenaline that perked him right up. An assault was trouble, right enough.

He was afraid there'd be another assault, too, when Hack jumped on Lawton for taking over the story. Much to Rhodes's surprise, it didn't happen.

He didn't ask why. He could come back to that later. Right now he had to find out about the assault and who'd handled it.

"Where did it happen?" he asked.

"At Wal-Mart," Lawton said.

"Wal-Mart?"

Another surprise. Wal-Mart wasn't the kind of place where assaults generally occurred, though of course Lige Ward had been known to chain himself to the doors there on more than one occasion before his unfortunate demise.

"That's right, Wal-Mart, right there just inside the front door."

"Who investigated?" Rhodes asked.

"Ruth," Hack said, finally getting in a word. "Henry pulled her car out of the ditch and brought it in, so I thought she might as well go."

Rhodes knew that Ruth could handle herself, but he would have thought Buddy a more likely candidate to check out an assault case.

"Who got assaulted?" he asked.

"Didn't say it was a who," Lawton told him.

"What?"

"That's right," Lawton said.

"What's right?"

"That's what I said."

Rhodes sank down in the chair at his desk. It had finally happened, just as he'd always been afraid that it would. His conversation with Lawton and Hack had finally turned into an Abbott and Costello routine.

He took a deep breath, and said, "Let me get this straight. There's been an assault at Wal-Mart. Is that right?"

"Right," Hack and Lawton said together.

"So far, so good. Now. Who got assaulted?"

"Not *who*," Lawton said. "What."

"What?"

"That's right."

And I-Don't-Know's on third, Rhodes thought. He wished he had a Dr. Pepper.

"Tell me what happened," he said. "From the beginning. Very slowly."

"I told you," Lawton said.

"Go over it again. But do a better job of it."

Lawton looked insulted. "Well, like I said, there was this assault at Wal-Mart."

"I got that much of it."

"On the crane machine," Hack said.

Rhodes finally figured it out. The assault hadn't been on a person, a *who*. It had been on a machine. A *what*.

"Why didn't you tell me that in the first place?" he asked.

"I thought I did," Lawton said. "What I said was—"

Rhodes held up his hand. "Never mind. Just go on with the story. Who assaulted the machine?"

"The Methodist preacher's kid," Lawton said. "You know how that machine works?"

"You put in a quarter or two quarters or whatever and turn the crank. The crane is supposed to drop down and pick up a prize. If you turn just right, it drops the prize in the slot, and the prize falls out. Not too many people can do it right, though."

"That's what the preacher's kid found out," Hack said.

"He shoulda known," Lawton said. "But maybe preachers' kids don't fool with those kinds of machines very much. Anyway, he took it pretty hard when he didn't get the prize he wanted. The witnesses that called it in said the kid kicked the machine and said a few words a preacher's kid ought not even to know."

"That's not much of an assault," Rhodes said.

"That ain't all," Hack told him. "The kid—"

"I'm tellin' this story," Lawton said, and to Rhodes's surprise, Hack didn't dispute him. "Anyway the kid, his name's Fisher, for Fisher of Men, prob'ly—"

"He was fishin' around in that slot," Hack said. "Maybe they named him *Fisher* for that."

Lawton glared at Hack, who shrugged and began inspecting the fingernails on his left hand.

"What happened then," Lawton said, "is that Fisher stood on some kind of a box and stuck his arm up in the slot, tryin' to grab the prize."

"And he couldn't get it out," Hack said. "His arm, that is. The prize, either. The box slipped out from under his feet, and he was sorta hangin' there—"

"And that's when he really started assaultin' the machine," Lawton said. "He was screamin' and kickin' and hammerin' on the plastic around all the prizes with the hand that wasn't stuck in the machine."

"But he was trapped by the machine," Rhodes said. "So it wasn't so much of an assault as an attempt to escape."

"You could call it that, I guess," Lawton said. "If you wanted to."

"Did they get his arm out?" Rhodes asked.

"Yeah," Lawton said. "Ruth called in and said that someone got some oil from the popcorn machine and they used that to grease his arm up. They finally got it out. He wasn't hurt much. Just a scraped arm."

"Maybe he's learned his lesson. Where's Ruth now?"

"She's on her way in," Hack said. "She'll be here in a minute."

"Good. Who took the call about the Wal-Mart thing, anyway?"

"Well, that was Lawton," Hack said. "He was sittin' in for me for a few minutes."

That explained why Hack had let Lawton tell most of the story. He hadn't been there when the call came in.

"Had to see his sweetie," Lawton said. "Had to go out to the café and have a little time together."

Hack had been keeping company with Mrs. McGee, a woman of his own age whom he'd met in the course of one of Rhodes's investigations.

"You're just jealous," Hack said. "Couldn't get a woman to look at you even if you won the Lotto."

"I'm better lookin' than some people I could name. I could get me a woman in a minute if I wanted one. It's just that I'd rather spend my time doin' my job than sparkin' some old lady."

"Don't you call Miz McGee an old lady," Hack said, starting to rise from his chair.

Rhodes said, "I think you'd better go check on the prisoner, Lawton. We want to be sure Nellie's comfortable during his stay here."

Lawton scowled at Hack for a minute and then turned toward the door leading to the cells.

"Did you check on the computer about gun sales?" Rhodes asked Hack.

"You asked me to, didn't you? But it didn't do any good, just like I told you. Nobody involved with the coaches bought any guns. Here's a printout just in case, though."

He handed Rhodes a piece of paper, and the sheriff glanced down the list of names and weapons. Hack was right. No one connected with the case had bought a pistol, and no one owned a .32. Everyone preferred a larger caliber.

He put the list aside as Ruth Grady came in the door. There was a dark stain on the front of her uniform.

"Popcorn oil," she said when she saw Rhodes looking at it. "Did Hack tell you about the little incident at Wal-Mart?"

"Hack and Lawton," Rhodes said. "Is the boy all right?"

"He's fine, and maybe he's learned a lesson."

"You can't count on it," Hack said. "Those preachers' kids are hard to deal with."

"We'll see about that later on, when he gets to be a teenager," Rhodes said.

"He won't be in town by then," Hack said. "Those Methodists move their preachers around a lot."

"Did you get a chance to talk to Bob Deedham and his wife?" Rhodes asked Ruth.

"I talked to him. She wasn't around."

"Did he say where she was?"

"No. Does it matter?"

"Not really." Rhodes said, though it might. Especially if she was out at The County Line. But that could wait until later. Right now, he wanted to hear what Deedham had to say.

He asked Ruth to tell him.

ELEVEN

IT WASN'T WHAT DEEDHAM had to say so much as the way he acted that interested Rhodes when Ruth gave her account.

Naturally Deedham had said there was no trouble between him and Brady Meredith. Rhodes wouldn't have expected anything different.

And Deedham had said that there was no relationship between Brady and Terry Deedham that he knew of. Of course she was an attractive woman, and there were bound to be rumors, but Deedham wasn't the kind of man who put any stock in talk like that.

Or so he said.

"He was nervous the whole time," Ruth told Rhodes. "He couldn't sit still. He'd get up and pace, and then he'd sit down for a minute. But he couldn't stay in the chair."

"Did he give any reason for being so jittery?" Rhodes asked.

"He said it was next week's game. He needed to be getting ready for it instead of talking to me. He said something about Springville's quarterback passing for three hundred yards last night and that he might be vulnerable to a blitz. He didn't seem concerned at all about Brady Meredith being dead, except how it might affect the game with Springville. That's pretty suspicious, if you ask me."

It seemed suspicious to Rhodes, too. It seemed to him that anyone would be more concerned about the murder of a colleague than a football game. Even in Texas.

"Did you ask him what he did after the game last night?"

"He claims that he worked at the field house until after one o'clock. He always stays to look at the game films after the other coaches have gone home. They all look at them together on Saturday morning, but Deedham watches them first. He's obsessed with football, all right."

Rhodes wondered if Deedham's obsession grew out of his relationship with his wife or vice versa.

"Anyone who can verify that he was there?"

"The managers were getting the gear stowed, he said, but they left before midnight."

So Deedham didn't have an alibi for most of the evening. Rhodes wasn't surprised.

"I don't suppose he mentioned where his wife was while he was at the field house."

"No," Ruth said. "I didn't ask him that."

"How about after he got home? Can she give us a time if we ask?"

"She was asleep when we got there. That's what he claims, at least. I got the impression that he didn't really know where she was."

Rhodes suspected that she had been at The County Line. He might be able to find out.

"Did you notice whether he smoked?" he asked.

"He didn't light up when I was there, but there was an ashtray on the coffee table."

Maybe Deedham didn't smoke, Rhodes thought. But he wasn't the only member of the household. Maybe Terry Deedham was the smoker. And maybe she even smoked Marlboros.

"Were there any butts in the ashtray?" he asked.

"No. It was clean."

Too bad. Rhodes was definitely going to have to pay a visit to Terry Deedham. But not tonight. He'd talk to her tomorrow unless she was in church when he went by. Somehow he didn't think she would be. From all he'd heard, she wasn't the churchgoing kind.

RHODES WAS GETTING dressed the next morning when the doorbell rang. His visitor was Jack Parry, the county judge, who, by virtue of his office, presided over the Commissioner's Court. He was, in effect, Rhodes's boss, though he usually didn't act like it.

"It's a fine day, isn't it," Parry said as he stood in the doorway.

He was a stout, bald man who was always smiling. He had worn a beard for years, but he had shaved it off before the last election. Now that the election was safely over and he was established in office, he had let it grow out again. It made him look older, but looking older wasn't a bad thing in his case. He was wearing a dark blue suit, white shirt, and a striped tie. And as usual, he was smoking a big cigar.

"It's a fine day, all right," Rhodes said. "Just about perfect."

The clouds and rain of the previous day had disappeared completely, leaving the sky a pale, empty blue. The pecan trees in Rhodes's yard cast sharp black shadows on the sidewalk and yard.

"Why don't we talk outside, Dan?" Parry said. "I don't want to smell up your house with this cigar."

Rhodes didn't mind the smell. It seemed to him much more pleasant than the smell of cigarettes, but Ivy might object.

"All right," Rhodes said, stepping out on the porch. "What brings you by today?"

"I was just on my way to church, Dan, when I thought about stopping by to say hello."

Rhodes didn't believe that for a second. Parry had never stopped by to say hello before, and as far as Rhodes knew he went to church every week. It wouldn't do to accuse the judge of lying, however, so Rhodes went along with him.

"That was thoughtful of you, Judge. I'll tell Ivy you came by."

"How is Ivy these days?" Parry asked. "You two happy? I'd like to think I tied the knot right."

Parry had married Rhodes and Ivy in the courthouse. Rhodes hadn't wanted any bigger ceremony than was absolutely necessary.

"You did a good job," Rhodes said, wondering when Parry would get to the point.

"I'm glad to hear it."

Parry took a puff of his cigar and blew smoke out toward Rhodes's lawn. He looked down at his suit and brushed the front of it. There weren't any ashes on the suit that Rhodes could see.

"About this Brady Meredith thing, Dan," Parry said.

Rhodes should have known. Parry was a big football fan. What else would have brought him by?

"What do you want to know?" Rhodes asked.

"Well, you know that I don't like to tell you how to do your job. I've never meddled in any of your cases before, have I?"

"No," Rhodes said. "You haven't."

"And I hate to start now." Parry leaned out over the porch railing and tapped on his cigar. "But this is serious."

"Most murders are," Rhodes said.

Parry nodded. "Of course. But this one is a little different from most. This one involves the football team. You know that we have a good chance to get to the state finals this year, don't you?"

"So I've been told."

"That would mean a lot to this town, Dan. We don't have much to be proud of these days, if you've noticed. Lots of stores downtown are closed: most of the place is just vacant buildings. Hardly any cotton farms left in the whole county. There's the power plant down the highway, but that's about it for industry. We need something to put some spirit back in this place, and the football team's doing that."

"I've noticed."

"I'm sure you have. People are talking about it everywhere. Did you read Goober's article about the game in the newspaper yesterday?"

Rhodes had read it after getting home. It was full of praise for Clearview's "outstanding defensive play," "quality linebacking corps," "formidable offensive line," and "strong-armed quarterback." It was almost as if Vance typed it on a cliché machine.

"Wonderful stuff," Parry said, puffing his cigar. "The town needs stories like that. But not stories like that other one."

Rhodes knew which one Parry meant—the one about Brady Meredith's murder.

"A real downer," Parry said. "I'm afraid it might affect the morale of the team."

Rhodes didn't see how that could be avoided. Getting a group of teenagers to play together as a team required a delicate psychological touch, and the stability that Jasper Knowles and his assistants had achieved during the season was certain to be affected by Brady's death.

"But if you could bring this to a quick conclusion," Parry said, "then the team might get straightened out in time for the game next Saturday. How are things going so far?"

"It's only been a day. I'm doing what I can."

Parry brushed at his suit front again. "That's not quite good enough, Dan. I'm talking about clues. Suspects. Things like that. We need to put out one of those bulletins that says something like 'Sheriff Rhodes expects an arrest at any minute.'"

"We could do that," Rhodes said. "But it wouldn't be the truth."

"Surely you have some ideas."

"I do. But nothing solid yet. There are a lot of people involved, and several of them might have had motives to kill Meredith. In fact, I'm going to talk to the team later on today. Maybe one of them did it.''

''Jesus Christ, don't say something like that! You don't really believe that, do you?''

So far, Rhodes hadn't turned up any evidence of steroid use by the team that might account for violent behavior by one of the players off the field, but there could be other motives he wasn't yet aware of. However, he didn't want to go into that with Parry.

''The truth is that I don't know what to believe right now,'' he said. ''This could take a little time, Jack. You'll just have to trust me to do it right.''

Parry puffed his cigar for a few seconds, then said, ''I guess you're right, Dan. I shouldn't have tried to get mixed up in this in the first place. It's just that this football team means so much to everybody.''

Rhodes wondered what Parry would say if he told him about the possibility that Meredith had been gambling on the team's games and that the games might have to be forfeited. He probably wouldn't say anything. He'd just have a heart attack and die right there on Rhodes's front porch.

So Rhodes didn't tell him. They talked for a few minutes, with Rhodes continuing to assure Parry that everything would work out sooner or later, and then the judge left to go to church.

RHODES FIGURED THAT Hayes Ford would be a late riser, so he went to visit the Deedhams first.

Bob Deedham was already at the field house, going over the films again, according to his wife, Terry, who was at home. She came to the door in a purple housecoat and invited Rhodes in for a cup of coffee.

Rhodes didn't drink coffee in the normal course of things, but he decided to make an exception in this case. It didn't taste any better than he remembered. Besides that, it was hot and it burned his tongue. He would have much preferred a Dr. Pepper.

"You don't mind if I smoke, I hope?" Terry Deedham said.

They were sitting in the kitchen at a square wooden table with four yellow plastic place mats on it. There was a little basket of artificial yellow flowers in the middle of the table. The bright morning sun streamed in through a window over the stainless steel sink.

"I don't mind," Rhodes said. "It's your house."

Terry pulled a package of cigarettes and a lighter from a pocket in her robe. Marlboro. She lit one and exhaled a long, thin stream of smoke.

"Bob doesn't like for me to smoke in the house," she said. "But I tell him it's my house, too."

She had masses of tousled blonde hair, big blue eyes, and thin white hands. She was quite pretty even though she wasn't wearing any makeup, but Rhodes could see the fine lines at the corners of her eyes and mouth and coarse-looking dark areas under her eyes.

"Your husband is really involved with the football team, isn't he?" Rhodes said.

Terry grinned, revealing a chipped front tooth that made her face look more interesting.

"Tell me about it. I haven't seen him for more

than five minutes at a time since a month before the season started.''

"You don't like football much yourself?" Rhodes said.

Terry put her cigarette on the saucer by her coffee cup and looked at Rhodes.

"Let me tell you something, Sheriff. I used to like football a whole lot. I was a cheerleader in high school. I was the homecoming queen. I never dated anyone but football players in high school or college. I watched football games on TV—college games and the pros, too.

"But all that was before I married Bob. I knew he liked football, but I didn't know how much. He eats it and sleeps it. He never thinks about anything else. When *he* watches a game on TV, he tapes it so he can go over the crucial plays later on and analyze the way they worked. Around here, it's football twelve months of the year. That can get pretty old after a while. Everybody needs a break now and then.''

She picked up her cigarette, took a deep drag, and blew out a plume of smoke.

"So now you know about me and Bob and football. But I bet that's not why you came here.''

"Not exactly,'' Rhodes said.

He tried another sip of coffee. It was cooler, but it didn't taste any better. He set the cup down, clinking it against the saucer. He didn't think he'd try it again. Enough was enough.

"It's about me and Brady, isn't it?'' Terry said.

"That's right," Rhodes said. "Do you want to tell me about you two?"

Terry crushed her cigarette in the saucer and lit another one.

"There's not much to tell. I liked Brady, but he didn't like me." She smiled reflectively. "That's not really true. He *liked* me, but he liked that mousy little wife of his more, if you can believe that. Are you married, Sheriff?"

Rhodes said that he was.

She nodded. "It figures. The cute ones always are."

"So are you," Rhodes pointed out.

"True. But in my case it hardly matters. '

"Why's that?"

"Because I'm not a football. If I were. maybe Bob would pay more attention to me."

"How would he feel if someone else paid a little attention to you?"

"You mean Brady? I doubt that Bob would even notice, no matter who it was."

"He noticed, all right. He saw the two of you at The County Line."

"What? Bob was spying on me? You don't mean that!"

Rhodes told her about his chat with Zach, the bartender.

Terry lit her third cigarette. There was a gray haze hanging around the ceiling fixture above the table.

"You wouldn't happen to have any Dr. Pepper, would you?" Rhodes said. He tapped his still-full coffee cup. "I'm not really much of a coffee drinker."

"I'll see." Terry got up and looked in the refrigerator. "Sorry. Just an old bottle of Pepsi. Will that do?"

"That's all right," Rhodes said. He already had one of the Marlboro butts in his pocket. "I don't need anything."

"Zach is sure it was Bob he saw?" Terry asked when she sat back down.

"He's sure. But come to think of it, he didn't actually say that Bob saw you and Brady. He just said that you two were on the dance floor and that Bob was in the bar."

"Damn. That's about the only time I was ever even able to get Brady to dance with me. Usually he'd have a couple of beers and then he was out of there. I think he just danced with me because he was feeling sorry for me."

"Maybe Bob didn't see you. But why would he have been there if he wasn't looking for you?"

"He saw me, all right. He'd never say it, though. I'm just surprised that he cared enough to follow me. Maybe he does care about something besides football."

"Were you at The County Line on Friday night?" Rhodes asked.

"Yes. And before you ask, I'm sure plenty of people saw me there; not everybody thinks football is the only thing in the world. I'm sorry Brady's dead; he was a nice guy. I sure didn't kill him."

"Did you go to the game before you went to The County Line?"

"No." Terry waved smoke away from her face. "I don't go to the games anymore. I've seen enough football to last me a lifetime."

Rhodes could have given her a little lecture, using Velma Knowles as an example, about wives who shared their husbands' interests, but he didn't think it was his place to do it. And Terry had a right to her own life, after all. Maybe Bob was the one who needed the lecture.

"What time did you get home?" Rhodes asked.

"I told you that I didn't kill Brady. Don't you believe me?"

"I don't know what to think right now," Rhodes said.

"Well, I didn't kill him. And Bob didn't either, if that's what you've been trying to get me to say. He might have followed me to The County Line, but I'm still not sure I believe that. And even if he did, he wouldn't kill anybody because he was jealous. He's not the least bit jealous. He hardly even knows I'm around."

"What time did Bob come in on Friday night?" Rhodes asked.

"I don't know. He always comes in late, but he never wakes me. I keep telling you—he's just not interested."

"But he came in after you did?"

"Yes. And before you ask, I came in at two o'clock. Or somewhere in there."

Deedham had told Ruth that he left the field house

around one o'clock. That left an hour of his time unaccounted for. It was an hour unaccounted for in Terry's case as well. Rhodes asked a few more questions, but he didn't get any more information. Terry Deedham stood in the kitchen door and waved goodbye when he left.

TWELVE

HAYES FORD LIVED pretty well for a man with no visible means of support.

Several years earlier he had bought one of the few real mansions in Clearview, built during the days when a few of the citizens were getting rich from the oil that lay in pools under the county, which were now mostly depleted. The house looked vaguely like a miniature version of a Spanish castle, with two whitewashed turrets topped by red tile and a white-walled courtyard in front.

The black wrought-iron gates of the courtyard were open. No one in Clearview worried much about locking up. Rhodes drove right in and parked by some spiky-leafed yucca plants. He walked up to the front doors, massive wooden portals that would have looked just fine on the front of an old Spanish mission. There was no doorbell, but on the right-hand door there was a heavy brass knocker shaped like a cowboy boot. Rhodes lifted the boot and pounded it on the plate beneath.

No one came to the door. Rhodes looked at his watch. Ten o'clock. It might still be a little early for Ford to be waking up. Rhodes pounded again.

There was still no response, and Rhodes looked to his left at the garage. The door was up and Ford's black Lexus was parked inside. Rhodes wondered idly how the Lexus drove. He wasn't likely ever to be able to afford one himself.

After pounding the knocker again and again getting no answer, Rhodes walked over to the garage. The Lexus was a little muddy, but it still had a shine.

Rhodes went around to the front of the car and put his hand on the hood. It was cold, which meant that Ford had been home for a while. Surely he had his nap out by now. Maybe he just didn't want any visitors.

Rhodes noticed a door leading from the garage into the house. There was a glass panel in the top of the door, but a curtain was hung over the panel on the inside. However, there was a lighted doorbell button beside the door. Rhodes pushed the button and the light went out. He could hear the doorbell echo inside the house. Two notes—one high, one low.

He waited for a moment, looking inside the Lexus while he did. Leather interior. Rhodes wondered if the leather wasn't uncomfortably hot in the summer and cold in the winter. Probably not cold, he thought. Probably the Lexus had heated seats.

He rang the doorbell again, waited again. He was getting tired of looking at the Lexus. It was a nice car, but Rhodes wanted to talk to Ford.

He tried the knob of the door. As he expected, it didn't move. Locked. Rhodes walked back around to the front. That door was locked as well.

Obviously Ford didn't want company. Or maybe he already had company and just didn't want anyone to intrude.

Or maybe there was another reason. Rhodes was

getting a bad feeling in the pit of his stomach. Unfortunately, a bad feeling in the stomach wasn't a good enough reason for a representative of the law to enter someone's residence.

Rhodes returned to the garage. In the rear wall there was a screen door that opened into the back yard. Rhodes pushed through the door and went around the back of the house to look for another entrance.

There was a semicircular patio with a glass-topped umbrella table sitting in the middle. Beyond the table a sliding glass door led into the house. A heavy curtain hung over the door, so Rhodes couldn't see inside.

Rhodes wasn't interested in seeing inside by now. He wanted to *get* inside, and the sliding door was perfect for his purposes, as any burglar could have told Hayes Ford. Such a door was almost impossible to lock effectively, and the old trick of laying a broomstick in the track didn't work very well either.

The fact of the matter was that sliding doors were generally installed by being lifted up and set onto a track. They could be removed the same way, easily and quickly, if you knew what you were doing.

Rhodes knew what he was doing, but he tried the door first. It was surprising how many people forgot to flip the flimsy lock, but Ford had remembered. Rhodes now had two choices: He could turn around and leave, or he could break in.

He wasn't going in with the intention of making an illegal search, but that didn't matter. Breaking into someone's house was still a crime, even if you were the sheriff.

Rhodes didn't care. The feeling that something was wrong was getting stronger, and he could always argue that he suspected that a crime had been committed on the premises if anyone asked him. No one was going to ask, anyway, if Hayes Ford was dead inside the house.

It took Rhodes about ten seconds to get the sliding door off its track and set it aside. In fact, it was even easier than it should have been, which could mean that someone had already done the same thing and loosened the door.

Or maybe I'm just getting paranoid, Rhodes thought. He pushed the curtain out of his way and entered the house.

Rhodes looked around the room, knowing that he was going to be embarrassed if Ford was upstairs with a girlfriend. The room was furnished with heavy carved wooden furniture that looked very uncomfortable.

"Anybody home?" Rhodes yelled.

His voice echoed off the high stucco ceiling and tile floor. There was no answer to his question, and he walked out of the room into a large foyer that led to the wooden doors at the front of the house. On his right was the kitchen. On his left were a hallway and the stairs leading to the second floor.

On the theory that the bedrooms would be upstairs, Rhodes started climbing.

"Ford? Are you up there?" he called.

No one called back. Rhodes stopped on the land-ing. Ford's car was in the garage, but no one appeared to be in the house. That wasn't right.

Rhodes didn't want to go on up the stairs. He was afraid of what he was going to find. But of course he went up anyway.

There was a hallway at the top of the stairs with three doorways on the left side. One of the doors was open.

"Ford?" Rhodes said, walking slowly toward the open door.

There was a king-size bed in the room. It had red satin sheets. There was a mirror on the ceiling that Rhodes strongly suspected hadn't been installed there by the original owners, who had been staunch Presbyterians.

The current owner, Hayes Ford, was staring wide-eyed at his reflection in the mirror as he lay on his back on the right side of the bed. He was wearing a red robe that gapped open over white satin boxer shorts with red hearts on them. The hearts matched the sheets, but Ford didn't care. He didn't care about anything. He was dead.

Rhodes took a deep breath and let it out slowly as he looked over the scene. He'd never liked Ford, and he'd tried to put him out of business more than once, but seeing the gambler like that made him feel sad and angry at the same time.

He should have locked those gates, Rhodes thought, but it was far too late to do anything about it now.

THE ONLY INTERESTING fact about Hayes Ford's murder, which Rhodes discovered after a careful search of the house, was that Ford had been shot in the head with a small-caliber gun. If Ford had been alive to take the wager, Rhodes would have bet him that the bullet came from the same pistol that had killed Brady Meredith.

The search itself had been interesting, however. One of the upstairs rooms had been converted into an office, complete with desk and computer. But there were no computer disks that Rhodes could find. He knew just enough about the machine to turn it on and discover that the hard drive had been disabled. Someone had made sure that there were no records available of Ford's activities.

Despite Rhodes's virtual certainty that Ford's murder was connected with the death of Brady Meredith, there was no way yet to prove the relationship. Judging from the condition of Ford's body, the gambler had been dead for about five or six hours, meaning that he had probably been killed not long after arriving home from wherever he had been on Saturday night. He'd probably been getting ready for bed when he was shot, but Rhodes couldn't be sure about that. He would have to wait until after the autopsy.

Things were getting complicated, the way they always seemed to when murder was involved, but at least Rhodes could remove Ford from his list of suspects in Meredith's killing. It was too bad, however, that Ford had to die to prove his innocence.

Or maybe Ford wasn't in the clear even now. There was no need to get in a hurry about it. What if Ford *had* killed Meredith and someone else had killed Ford? That was certainly possible. For that matter, there didn't have to be any connection between the deaths at all.

But Rhodes didn't believe in coincidence in cases like this. There was a connection, all right. He just had to find it.

RHODES, HAVING MISSED lunch yet again, was a little late in getting to the field house. Jasper Knowles must have assumed that Rhodes wasn't coming; Jerry Tabor was addressing the team.

Tabor was wearing his letter jacket and a Clearview Catamount cap. The patches that lined the jacket's leather sleeves indicated that Tabor had been chosen for the all-district team, the all-region team, and the all-state team. The cap was much newer than the jacket, and it covered Tabor's bald spot.

Rhodes stood unobtrusively in the back of the room and listened to Tabor's speech.

"I want you to remember one thing," Tabor said. His voice sounded a little hollow in the large room. "Every game you win from here on in is something you'll have forever. Every one of them will give you a feeling like nothing else you've ever had and like nothing else you'll ever experience. When you come back to your twenty-fifth-year class reunion, you'll look at each other, and you'll feel that special feeling all over again. It's something nobody will ever be able to take away from you, no matter what happens."

It was sentimental but true. As much as Rhodes

tried to downplay his days as the Will-o'-the-Wisp, he'd never forgotten the thrill of making that run.

On the other hand, it wasn't something he thought about all the time, and he wasn't sure that anyone else really remembered it, even Ivy, who was about the only one who ever brought it up, and she was usually joking.

Tabor, on the other hand, evidently took his glory days seriously and thought about them often, especially now that the team's winning season was helping people to recall his brief interval of celebrity. To be fair about it, though, his interval had been a lot longer than Rhodes's.

Nevertheless, Rhodes didn't think it was a good idea to tell high school kids that they were having the best experience of their lives by getting into the play-offs. It didn't give them much to look forward to as adults.

"And it's just going to get better," Tabor continued. "Every game, it gets better. Bi-district, regional, all the way to state." He paused and looked around the room. "Now, I never made it to state myself, but you're going all the way. No doubt about it. Nothing can stop you!"

The team members stomped and whistled and cheered and bounced around in their chairs. The coaches applauded, Bob Deedham more enthusiastically than the others.

"That's right," Tabor said. "You're going all the way! And when you come back to that twenty-five-year reunion, you'll look in each other's eyes, and you won't even have to say a word. You'll look older, even if you can't believe that now. Some of you'll have gray hair. Some of you won't have much hair at all.''

He took off his cap and rubbed his bald spot. Some of the players laughed, and he settled the cap back on his head.

''You might not have quite the energy you used to, and your bellies won't be near as flat as they are now. But it won't matter! When you see the men you shared this experience with, they'll still look the same to you, and you'll still look the same to them. It'll be like all those years never even happened. They'll just drop away, and you'll be Catamounts again!''

Tabor's voice cracked. There were more cheers, stomps, and whistles.

Tabor had to wait for a few seconds after the noise died down before he got control of himself.

''You're such a great bunch of guys,'' he said. ''You deserve this, and I want you to know how much I appreciate you and the coaches letting me share it with you.''

''You're one of us, Jer'!'' someone yelled, and the cheering started again.

''Naw,'' Tabor said when things were calm again. ''I was good, but I was never as good as you guys!''

More cheers. It was almost as good as a brush-arbor revival meeting, Rhodes thought. He wondered why Tabor wasn't more successful at selling used cars. If he could get to his customers the way he was getting to the Catamounts, the whole town of Clearview would be driving around in cars with little chrome "Del-Ray Chevrolet" signs stuck to the trunk.

"Now," Tabor said, his voice lowering, "there's something else you have to think about. Coach Meredith."

He paused, but there weren't any cheers this time. Just dead silence in the room. Rhodes could hear the click of the thermostat just before the heat came on. Warm air poured out of the ceiling vents.

"We all remember Coach Meredith," Tabor said. "And we always will. We'll remember what a great guy he was, what a fine gentleman. We'll remember how much he taught us about the game. How much he taught us about sportsmanship and character."

Rhodes thought that last was a pretty peculiar remark, considering that Meredith had recently tried to punch out the head coach, but the team didn't seem to think so. They sat quiet and still, waiting for Tabor to continue.

"But we can't let his death stop us. We've got to go on. That's the way he'd want it, and all of you know it. He wouldn't want us to quit on him now. He'd want us to go out there and play our very best. He'd want us to go right on to that state championship game, and he'd want us to win it! And that's all I'm really talking about here. I want us to win this week and to go on winning until we get to that big game. And I want us to win that one for Coach Meredith!"

While Rhodes was trying to figure out just exactly when Tabor had lapsed into the first person, the room erupted in cheering. The team members jumped out of their chairs, pounding each other on the back, giving high fives, and elbowing each other out of the way for the chance to shake Tabor's hand.

Tabor couldn't have done it any better if Meredith had been the Gipper, and Rhodes noticed that Bob Deedham had a satisfied smile on his face. He wondered if Deedham had helped Tabor with the speech.

The players were still milling around the room and around Tabor when Jasper Knowles finally noticed Rhodes. He made his way through the team and came over to the sheriff.

"I sure hate for you to have to talk to the boys now," he said. "They're feelin' too good to have you question them about Brady."

"I don't think I'll bother them, then," Rhodes said. What with the new murder, he wasn't sure he needed to.

"I sure appreciate that, Sheriff," Knowles said. He looked back at the celebration. "I didn't mean for Jerry to bring up Brady, though. I don't think it's right to use a man like that after he's dead."

"I know," Rhodes said. "I heard you tell Deedham yesterday."

"Bob's that way, though. He'd use his own grandmother if it'd get him another win. Maybe that's what coachin's all about, but I never felt that way, myself. Anyway, you don't want to hear about that. Have you found out anything new about the murder?"

Rhodes told him about Hayes Ford.

"Lord knows, that's awful! Who did it?"

"I don't know yet. But I suspect it's tied to Brady some way or another."

Knowles looked over at Kenner and Deedham, who were now talking to Jerry Tabor.

"You don't think any of us had anything to do with it, do you?"

"I don't know what to think," Rhodes said. "When I do, I'll let you know. Right now, I just want to talk to Roy Kenner for a minute."

"Roy? He didn't know Hayes Ford."

"Maybe not. But I have to talk to him anyway."

"There's a room right over there, then," Knowles said. "You want me to send him over?"

"You might as well," Rhodes said.

THIRTEEN

"AND YOU DON'T THINK Roy Kenner had an affair with Terry?" Ruth Grady asked Rhodes.

Rhodes told her he didn't think so. They were in his office in the courthouse, the one he rarely used. It provided a lot more privacy than the jail, however, especially on Sunday, when no one else was in the building, and Rhodes didn't want to be interrupted. To make up for missing lunch, he was drinking a Dr. Pepper and eating some crackers and peanut butter that he'd gotten from a vending machine.

"Roy admitted that he actually went out with her a time or two," Rhodes said. "Which is more than Brady Meredith ever did, if we can trust his wife. But Roy says that's all it amounted to. He just took her dancing."

"At The County Line?"

"Roy's not that dumb." Rhodes took a drink of Dr. Pepper. "He took her all the way to the next county. He didn't want to run into anyone he knew. Like Brady."

"So where does that leave us?" Ruth asked.

Rhodes honestly didn't know. "Here's what I thought at first. There were three reasons why someone might have killed Brady Meredith. One was jealousy; Bob Deedham qualified. I'm not so sure he still doesn't.

"The second one was money. Maybe he was surprised to have shaved some points in the game. Ford would have paid him off for that, but he didn't get to do it. Knowles overruled him. So Ford either killed him or had him killed. I have to admit that one wasn't too likely, since Ford doesn't seem like the type to kill anybody. He might have it done, though."

"By somebody like Rapper," Ruth said.

"That's right. Or Rapper could have been involved in the third plot I worked out, the one where Brady was feeding steroids to the team. But that doesn't seem very likely now. Brady didn't like drugs in any form."

Rhodes ate his last cracker and threw the crinkly plastic wrapper in the trash can.

"That still left me with a couple of theories, though. Jasper Knowles and Brady had been having trouble all year, but after I talked to Jasper, I ruled him out. He didn't seem especially upset with Brady. He wasn't as upset as his wife was."

"And now that Ford is dead, we have a whole new ball game," Ruth said.

"That's right. Now we have to fit him into it for sure. Do you have any ideas?"

Ruth hesitated. "Do they have to be new ideas?"

"The old ones are fine," Rhodes said. "*If* they can fit the new situation."

"OK. How about this: Brady wasn't feeding steroids to anyone. Someone else was, and Brady found out. That's why he was killed."

"That might fit Rapper back into things," Rhodes

said. "And it might even fit with another idea that I didn't mention, that one of the team got a little hyped up on drugs and killed his coach. I didn't ever like that one very much, but it's still possible. It doesn't explain Ford, though."

"So maybe it all goes back to the gambling. Have you got any way to find out more about that?"

"I can talk to Clyde Ballinger, but he wasn't much help the first time. It might be a good idea to talk to some of the other Catamount Club members."

"How about this idea," Ruth said. "Brady Meredith wanted to give up gambling, or maybe pay off his bets with Ford. One way to do that would be to blackmail some of Ford's other clients. That might help explain the missing records."

"Brady killed Ford and stole the records, then someone else killed Brady?"

"Why not?"

"Because Ford was killed about twenty-four hours after Brady."

"All right, try this. The client killed Brady to stop the blackmail, then killed Ford to get the records and make sure no one tried it again."

"What kind of customer would pay blackmail?" Rhodes asked. "Ford wasn't a big-timer. He didn't take any bets for over a thousand dollars or so."

"Someone who had a lot to lose would pay. Is there anyone like that around town? What about in the Catamount Club?"

Rhodes couldn't think of anyone, but it wouldn't hurt to look into that angle.

"You take Gerald Bonny and Ron Tandy," he said. "I'll talk to the others."

"Oh, fine. Give me the lawyer."

"Gerald's easy to talk to, and he's made a lot of money lawyering. Tandy's been selling real estate for years. They're the ones most likely to have the money, and maybe even something to lose. I'm not sure how much good it would do either of them if people knew they were betting on high school games."

Ruth got up. "Well, we'll see. Shall I go by the jail after I'm done?"

"That's a good idea. Don't take any calls from Hack before you're finished, either. Tell him to get Buddy instead."

"All right. Before I go, tell me one thing."

"What's that?" Rhodes asked.

"Is there anyone mixed up in all this that you suspect more than the others?"

"Bob Deedham," Rhodes said.

"Why?"

"Because I don't like him much." Rhodes had to laugh at himself. "That's not a very good reason, is it?"

"It's about as good as anything else we've got," Ruth said.

After she was gone, Rhodes drank the last of his Dr. Pepper and telephoned Clyde Ballinger. Ballinger didn't want to come to the courthouse, but Rhodes reminded him that it was much more private than anywhere else they could talk.

"I don't know what else I can tell you," Ballinger said.

"We'll talk about that when you get here."

"Damn," Ballinger said. "OK. I'll be there in fifteen minutes."

"I'll be waiting," Rhodes said.

BALLINGER WASN'T HAPPY when he arrived.

"I know what this is about," he said. "And I told you that I didn't do any betting with Hayes Ford, and I didn't kill him, either."

"I didn't say you did," Rhodes told him.

"Well, it's a good thing. Because I didn't."

"You didn't happen to bring a report from Dr. White, did you?" Rhodes asked.

Ballinger's anger left him all at once. He reached in his coat pocket.

"I did." He put the report on Rhodes's desk. "I thought you might need it."

Rhodes glanced through the report. As he'd suspected, Ford had been shot with a .32, just like Meredith. He'd get a comparison made between the bullets, but he thought he already knew what the final report would tell him. He also learned that Ford had been dead about eight hours and had just brushed his teeth before he was killed.

"Two murders," Rhodes said. "You can see why I might need a little information."

"I can see, all right." Ballinger sat down across from Rhodes. "But I just don't have any."

"Maybe you know more than you think. You said

that nobody in the Catamount Club ever bet very much. Are you sure about that?''

''I'm not sure, but if anyone did, it was kept pretty quiet.''

''What would the reason for that be?''

''You mean why keep it quiet? You know that as well as I do. This is a small town, and it's all right if there's one gambler around. But respectable people don't gamble. They get in football pools, like I said, and they might play the Lotto when there's a big prize, but they don't bet real money. That's for crooks.''

''So if people found out that someone like Gerald Bonny had lost a few thousand dollars to Hayes Ford, they might just take their law business to someone else.''

''Probably. You don't want some loser gambler drawing up your will.''

''Or selling you a house?''

''No. But Gerald and Ron didn't kill anybody.''

''How do you know?''

Ballinger started to answer, then stopped to think about it. ''Well, maybe they would. But I don't *think* they would. I guess that's why you're the sheriff and I'm just the undertaker.''

Rhodes hadn't heard anyone use the word *undertaker* in years, even before people had become politically correct.

''I thought you were a funeral director,'' he said.

''All right, funeral director. That wasn't what I meant.''

"I know," Rhodes said. "What do you think about Jerry and Tom and Jimmy?"

"I think they're about as likely to be killers as I am. And I'm not likely."

"I feel pretty much the same way," Rhodes admitted. "I was hoping that you'd come in and tell me that you'd thought it over and that you know about some big money changing hands."

Ballinger shrugged. "If I could help you, I would. But I don't know a thing."

Rhodes tapped the report on the desk. "Thanks for bringing this over to me. If you think of anybody who might have had it in for Hayes Ford, give me a call."

"You find somebody who's lost a lot of money to him, then you'll have the killer," Ballinger said. "Not somebody who's lost just once. Somebody who's lost consistently."

There was something in that idea, and Rhodes thought about it after Ballinger had gone. Somebody who was partners with Brady Meredith, say, might have a reason to kill both Meredith and Ford, Meredith for not having shaved the points, and Ford for getting a little too eager to collect.

Rhodes spent the rest of the afternoon turning it over in his mind, but he didn't come up with anything. There were so many ways of putting the puzzle together that he couldn't make it fit into any reasonable shape.

There were even a few pieces that he couldn't fit in at all with his gambling theories, and one of them was Rapper. Nellie had already bonded out, so

Rhodes couldn't question him, and Rapper was no-where to be found.

Maybe his presence in Blacklin County at this par-ticular time was just an accident, but Rhodes didn't think so. He didn't think it was any more of a co-incidence than anything else that was happening. He just couldn't fit it into the puzzle.

The courthouse was always quiet, though sounds echoed off its marble floors and walls. But on Sun-days it was like a tomb, cold and dark. Rhodes thought he might be better off if he went somewhere else to think.

As he walked to his car, he regretted not having talked to the football team. If there was any truth at all in the rumors about steroids, the team was where he'd most likely find the answers. Well, he didn't need Jasper Knowles's permission to talk to anyone. After all, he was the sheriff. He could go by and talk to some of the players at home, and he might as well start with Jay Kelton, the one who'd made the out-of-bounds tackle.

THE KELTONS LIVED in a house that was a lot dif-ferent from the one Hayes Ford had bought with his gambling money. It was more like Rhodes's own house, a wood-frame building that was well-maintained but that had seen better days.

There was a large white sign with blue and gold lettering in the front yard. It said;

A FIGHTING CLEARVIEW CATAMOUNT LIVES HERE!

YEA, JAY!
HE'S GREAT—NO. 38!

There were similar signs in the yards of every player on the team. The cheerleaders painted them before the season and drove around town in a pickup truck unloading them at the players' homes. Rhodes wasn't sure that all of them had little rhymes on them, though maybe they did.

He knocked on the front door. The knock was answered by Mr. Kelton, who asked Rhodes to come in. He was taller than Rhodes and fencepost thin. He was holding the Sunday comics section of some big-city paper in his hand, and he was wearing a pair of reading glasses that Rhodes suspected came from Lee's drugstore, or maybe Wal-Mart.

"Martha's back in the kitchen, cooking supper," Kelton said. "What's going on, Sheriff? Is this about that restraining order the Garton coaches were going to get against us?"

The smell of frying chicken almost made Rhodes weak in the knees. The peanut butter and crackers he'd eaten earlier hadn't done much in the way of satisfying his hunger.

"It's not the restraining order," he said. "I'd like to talk to Jay for a few minutes if I could," he said.

"Is it about the coach?"

"Yes, sir, it is. But Jay's not involved in that." Rhodes hoped he was telling the truth. "This is something that has to do with the team."

"What about the team?"

"It's just a rumor I've heard," Rhodes said. "I'd

rather just talk to your son about it and then let him tell you if he wants to.''

Kelton plainly wanted to know more, but he said, ''Well, I guess that would be all right. He's in his room. I'll call him.''

''Don't do that,'' Rhodes said. ''I'd rather talk to him in his room if you'd just show me the way.''

They crossed the den and turned down a short hall. Kelton tapped lightly on a door with the tip of his index finger and waited. When there was no answer, he pounded on the door with the heel of his right hand.

''Headphones,'' he said.

Rhodes nodded, and in a moment the door opened. Jay Kelton stood there with a questioning look on his face. He was as tall as his father, but his shoulders were wider. He was wearing a tight Clearview T-shirt, and Rhodes could see that he'd been doing a lot of weight training. There was a scab on the bridge of his nose, and Rhodes wondered if he'd gotten scratched when he made the late hit on the Garton player. His stomach was flat as a plate, for which Rhodes envied him just a little, even though he knew that Jerry Tabor had been right about that: When Jay came back to his twenty-five-year reunion, his stomach wouldn't be nearly as flat as it was now.

''What's up?'' Jay asked. A pair of headphones hung around his neck, and Rhodes could hear the faint strains of music coming from them.

''The sheriff wants to talk to you,'' Kelton said. ''He'll tell you what it's about.''

''In your room if you don't mind,'' Rhodes said.

"Sure," Jay told him. "Come on in."

Rhodes stepped through the door into the room. The walls were covered with posters that made Rhodes realize he had lost touch with the music world a long time ago, though he thought he might be able to name the category to which some of the bands displayed on the walls belonged. Hack, who kept up with that sort of thing for some reason, had explained it to him: "Matted hair, that's grunge. Teased hair, that's metal."

Then Rhodes saw that on one poster was a huge picture of the band Kiss. Maybe the world hadn't passed him by after all.

Or then again, maybe it had. Rhodes looked around the room. When he was growing up, Rhodes had never known a kid with his own telephone, much less his own TV set, his own computer, and his own CD player. Of course, *no one* had owned a computer or a CD player when Rhodes was growing up.

"You wanna sit down?" Jay asked, turning off the CD player and taking off the headphones.

The only chair in the room was at the computer desk. Rhodes pulled it out and sat in it. Jay sat on his twin bed, under a poster of Pearl Jam. *Grunge,* Rhodes thought, looking at the group's hair.

"You wanted to talk to me?" Jay asked.

He put the headphones on the desk. He had innocent brown eyes, and the kind of easygoing confidence that Rhodes had seen in a lot of young athletes, the kind of confidence that came from knowing that you were special, that you had skills that mattered, that everyone in your class looked up to you because of what you could do on a football field or on a basketball court. For some reason, kids who could balance a chemical equation or explain the binomial theorem usually didn't have that kind of confidence at all. Maybe it was because no one had ever put a sign in their yards.

"I wanted to ask you something about the team," Rhodes said. "Something that I hope you'll keep in confidence."

Jay slumped back against the wall, completely at ease. "I can keep a secret, sure."

Rhodes wished he believed him. In his experience, hardly anyone could keep a secret. But it didn't really matter; in fact, it might do some good if the team knew that someone was interested in finding out about steroids. It might put a little fear in them, if anything could, which was doubtful. And fear sometimes made people talk.

"I'm glad to hear it," Rhodes said. "Here's the problem. There's a rumor going around that some of the players have been using steroids."

Jay leaned forward. "That's a bunch of crap. Who told you that?"

"Nobody in particular. It's something that's going around, that's all."

"Well, it's crap. Why would anybody do that? It's crazy. Steroids turn your balls to wood. Everybody knows that."

Rhodes hadn't known that. He'd have to remember to avoid steroids at all costs. No need to take chances, even if it wasn't true.

"It has other effects, too," Rhodes said. "It helps

you bulk up. Builds up muscle, makes you a little more aggressive for the game.''

"Turns you into a maniac, that's what Coach Meredith always said. Man, he was always preachin' against drugs like that.''

Rhodes wondered if Meredith was the one who'd passed along the information about the effect of steroids on one's gonads. Oh, well. Whatever worked.

"Besides,'' Jay went on, "if the UIL caught anybody takin' a drug like that, we'd be out of the playoffs in about half a second. Probably have to forfeit all our games. Boy, those Garton assholes would love that!''

Young people these days were also considerably less inhibited in their language around their elders than Rhodes remembered his generation having been. While *assholes* would have been a perfectly acceptable word among one's peers, it would have been nearly impossible to say it in front of an adult. Jay Kelton, however, didn't even seem to notice that he'd said anything unusual.

"So no one that you know of takes steroids?'' Rhodes asked.

"That's what I've been sayin'.''

"And the coaches have never mentioned them?''

"I told you that Coach Meredith was always preachin' about them, didn't I?''

"Favorably, I meant.''

Jay's eyes flicked to Rhodes's left. Rhodes turned his head slightly and saw nothing more interesting than a Candlebox poster. He looked back at Jay, who was now meeting his eyes. But it was too late. Rhodes knew he was about to hear a lie.

"Nobody was ever favorable about drugs," Jay said. "That would be stupid."

Rhodes didn't know exactly what approach to take. There were some people who didn't take very well to being called liars, and Jay Kelton looked like one of them.

"What about Coach Deedham?" he asked.

"Who told you that?" Jay slid off the bed and stood up. "That's a damn lie. Coach Deedham never said a thing about any drugs, and I'll whip the one who says he did."

"I was just asking a hypothetical question," Rhodes said. "Let's just forget that I brought it up."

"Fine. Let's do that."

Jay sat back down on his bed and leaned against the wall. But this time his back was stiff and his arms were crossed in front of his chest. Rhodes was certain his sudden burst of hostility was inspired by a genuine feeling of outrage, not steroids.

"I'm glad to know that the coaches were so strongly against drugs," Rhodes said, getting out of the chair. "I thought it was just a false rumor, and it's good to hear the truth."

"Yeah," Jay said. "It was a false rumor."

"I appreciate your being so honest with me," Rhodes told him. "You can tell your father about this, but I hope you won't mention it to anybody else."

"I told you, I can keep a secret."

"That's right. Thanks for your help."

Rhodes left Jay scowling in his room, sitting under the Pearl Jam poster.

"Was the boy any help?" Mr. Kelton asked when Rhodes returned to the den.

"I think so," Rhodes said. "We'll see."

"Well, I sure hope you catch whoever it was that killed Coach Meredith. We've talked to Jay about it, tried to help him deal with it. He seems all right, but you never can tell."

Rhodes thought that in spite of their tendency to dramatize things, young people had a lot less trouble dealing with death than most adults thought.

"He seems fine," Rhodes said.

"We don't want him to be down for the game next weekend," Kelton said. "It's a big one."

Rhodes nodded. "That's right."

"Then there's that restraining order. I sure hate it that those Garton folks are such bad sports. I talked to Jay about that hit, and he says that he didn't know that boy was out of bounds. When you're running down the field full tilt that way, you've got your eye on the ball carrier, not on the sideline. There wasn't any reason for Jay to get thrown out of the game. I'm sorry there was a fight, but I sure don't think there's any need to carry this in front of some judge. I say let's keep football on the field and out of the courtroom."

Rhodes thought that was a pretty catchy saying, but he didn't think it would meet with much approval in Garton.

"From what I gather," he said, "There's not much likelihood of a judge ruling against the officials on a football game. I think you can rest easy about that.''

"I hope so. We don't need any more distractions.'' Kelton glanced over his shoulder toward the kitchen. "I think supper's about ready. You want a little fried chicken?"

The answer was yes, but Rhodes said. "No, thanks, I've got a lot of work to do. I appreciate the offer, though."

"Martha makes about the best fried chicken I've ever tasted," Kelton said. "I could snag you a piece to take with you."

"No, thanks," Rhodes said, hoping that his mouth wasn't watering too obviously. "I'll eat later."

"Well, you go on and catch whoever killed the coach, then. I think it'll be a big load off the team's mind when that's taken care of."

'I'm sure it will be," Rhodes said.

FOURTEEN

RHODES THOUGHT it was a little strange that while everyone seemed to want him to find Brady Meredith's killer, no one seemed to care much about Meredith himself. They wanted the killer found so the team wouldn't be affected for the big game, not because a man was dead or because they wanted to see justice done.

Rhodes also thought that he should have come up with the connection between Deedham and steroids a long time before now. Deedham was, after all, the one coach of the four whom everyone had said would do anything to win.

It had been obvious from the first that Deedham cared more about winning than he cared about Brady Meredith's death, more than he cared about his wife, more than he cared about anything or anyone. If a coach was encouraging the use of steroids, Deedham was the most likely candidate.

As Rhodes drove back to the jail, he thought about how different Deedham and Meredith were. On the one hand, there was Deedham, a coach who thought that winning was everything and would probably even give illegal drugs to his players in order to get a victory. On the other hand, there was Meredith, a coach who presumably liked winning—what coach didn't?—but who was so opposed to drugs that he didn't even like caffeine in soft drinks. There was certainly a potential for conflict between the two of them, maybe deadly conflict.

Rhodes wasn't too clear on what Deedham might actually have said or done about the steroids, and he knew that he could never have gotten the truth from Jay Kelton, but he had gotten close enough to it to draw some inferences.

Deedham had certainly mentioned steroids at one time or another if Rhodes had read Jay Kelton's reaction to his questions rightly, but whether any of the team members were actually taking the drugs was another question. Judging by what Rhodes had heard from Jay, it seemed that Meredith's philosophy had been influential enough to keep the Catamounts honest.

Rhodes hoped so, because Jay was right about one thing. If anyone were caught using drugs, the team would be out of the play-offs, and all the coaches would lose their jobs. It was too bad that Deedham would even consider such a risk, but Rhodes was convinced that he had.

So it was possible that Deedham had not been at The County Line to spy on his wife. Maybe he had been there to talk to Rapper instead.

The possibilities that opened out from that idea were endless. Meredith could have seen Deedham and Rapper, guessed their business, and confronted them. That might make Rapper the killer, but it didn't let out Deedham, who might have been angered because he'd seen Meredith with Terry.

Just exactly how Hayes Ford fit into that scenario, Rhodes wasn't sure. He'd have to work that out later.

When he arrived at the jail, Ruth's car was already there. The deputy was talking to Hack and Lawton when Rhodes went inside.

Before Rhodes could ask Ruth about her talks with Bonny and Ron Tandy, Hack said, "We got us a big shot in jail, Sheriff."

Rhodes looked at Ruth, who just grinned and rolled her eyes. Rhodes knew he was in for it then.

"What kind of big shot?" he asked.

"One of them bullfighters," Lawton said. "Buddy brought him in."

"He was drunk," Hack said, taking back the story. "Buddy found him wanderin' around out at the city park. Prob'ly went there when he realized he couldn't drive, and got out of his car for some reason or other—"

"Had to go to the bathroom, I bet," Lawton said. "His pants were unzipped when we locked him up."

"—but we don't know why," Hack continued as if Lawton hadn't spoken. "Buddy was takin' a short cut through the park and saw him wanderin' around over by the bandstand, couldn't hardly stand up. So Buddy went and tried to talk to him, and then he brought him in."

Rhodes had a lot of questions, but he was almost afraid to ask them.

"You say Buddy *tried* to talk to him?"

"That's right," Lawton said. "He tried, but he couldn't."

"Why not? Was the man too drunk to talk?"

"He wasn't too drunk," Hack said. "He just couldn't talk English. He's a *bullfighter.* They come from Mexico or maybe from Spain."

"And you say he's a big shot?"

"Sure he's a big shot. Famous, anyway."

"If you can't talk to him," Rhodes said, "how do you know he's famous?"

"He could tell us that much," Lawton said. "That's about all the English he could talk."

"But he said that he was a famous bullfighter?"

"That's right," Hack said. "Famous bullfighter. That's what *matador* means, ain't it? Bullfighter?"

"He said he was a famous matador?"

Hack looked first at Ruth and then at Lawton. "Ain't that what we been tellin' you all along?"

"That's what we been tellin' him," Lawton agreed.

"Isn't there a Mexican restaurant in Garton called The Famous Matador?" Rhodes asked.

Hack thought for a second. "By gosh, I believe you're right. Got a big sign out in front, a bullfighter with a neon cape that sorta waves back and forth."

"That's the place," Rhodes said. "I think I'd better have a talk with the prisoner."

RHODES SPOKE a little Spanish, enough to make himself understood most of the time, and he could understand more than he spoke. It didn't take him long to find out that the prisoner was from Garton and that he worked in the kitchen at The Famous Matador. His name was Jaime Saenz. He'd come to Clearview for the football game, met a young woman who spoke Spanish a lot better than either Rhodes or Buddy, and stayed in town for an extra couple of days.

He was desperate to get back to Garton, he said, because he was afraid he was going to lose his job at the restaurant. He'd been drunk that afternoon when Buddy found him, though maybe not as drunk as Buddy thought. The language barrier had no doubt compounded the problem. At any rate, he seemed sober now.

Rhodes went back downstairs and told Ruth that he was going to release the prisoner. She could take him back to the park for his car.

"What if he gets drunk again?" Ruth asked.

"Follow him until he leaves the county to make sure he doesn't," Rhodes told her. "We don't want him to lose his job, but we don't want him to have an accident, either."

"Can you hold him for a few more minutes? It won't take long for me to tell you about Bonny and Tandy."

"All right. What did you find out?"

She found out that both men had indeed bet with Ford and that both were eager to keep their involvement with the gambler a secret.

"It's not public opinion that they're worried about, though," she said. "Not in Bonny's case, anyway."

"What is it, then?"

"It's his wife. He wouldn't talk to me at his house. I had to meet him at his office. He's lost a little more money than he'd like for his wife to know about. In fact, I got the impression that *any* money he lost would be more than he'd like for her to know about."

"Does he have an alibi for last night?"

"He was with his wife. He says she can vouch for him, but he really doesn't want to have to bring her into it. If he does, she'll find out about the gambling."

"What do you think?"

"I don't think he murdered Ford," Ruth said. "Anybody who's that scared of his wife wouldn't kill somebody."

Rhodes wasn't sure that the theory made sense, but he'd known Bonny a long time. He didn't think Bonny was a killer, either.

"What about Tandy?" he asked.

"He says he's never made a bet over ten dollars in his life. He doesn't believe in it. He even went to Las Vegas last year just to see the shows."

Rhodes had known Tandy for a long time, too. There was a rumor around Clearview that he still had the first nickel he'd ever made, which was an exaggeration, but not too much of one. If he said he didn't bet excessively, Rhodes believed him.

"Of course, he's a deacon at First Baptist," Ruth said. "Nothing would happen to him if the congregation found out he'd bet with Ford, and probably nobody would even say anything about it to him. But they'd talk about it when he wasn't around, as he well knows, so he'd hate for the word to get out."

"We won't tell anyone unless we have to," Rhodes said. "Let me tell you about another angle on this mess."

He told Ruth about his talk with Jay Kelton and his theory about the steroids.

"It sounds like it might lead somewhere," she said. "What are you going to do about it?"

"I'm going to call Ivy to let her know I'll be late," he said. "And then I'm going to talk to Bob Deedham."

WHEN HE LEFT THE JAIL Rhodes didn't go straight to the Deedhams' house. He stopped at the H.E.B. and bought a can of Vienna sausages, a quarter-pound of mild cheddar cheese, and a box of whole-wheat crackers. A man could go only so long without food.

He opened the sausages in the parking lot and felt a mild twinge of guilt when he saw the congealed grease collected around the tops. The guilt passed when he ate one, however. He sliced through the plastic wrap of the cheese with his pocket knife and cut off a chunk. He put it on a cracker and ate it, hardly thinking of the fat grams. The crackers were whole wheat, he told himself. That had to count for something.

He ate all the sausages, but not all the cheese. And of course there were plenty of crackers left. He got a Dr. Pepper from the machine in front of the store and drank it as he drove to the Deedhams'.

He tried not to let the fact that he didn't like Bob Deedham influence his thoughts on the case, but it was hard not to. If he could prove a connection between Deedham and Rapper, he thought he would have a pretty good reason to suspect the two of them in Meredith's death. The problem was that he wouldn't have anything more than suspicion. There was no proof, and proof was what he had to have.

He was almost to the Deedhams' house when Hack called on the radio.

"Miz Wilkie just phoned," he said. "She said she heard motorsickles again and thought you'd want to know."

"When?" Rhodes asked.

"Just then," Hack said. "I called you soon as she hung up."

"I don't mean when did she phone. When did she hear the motorcycles?"

"Right before she phoned me. They were headin' toward town, she said."

"All right. I'll drive over toward Milsby and see what I can see."

"You be careful," Hack said.

"I always am. Has Ruth already gone to escort that famous bullfighter of yours home to Garton?"

"She just left. If you want some backup, I can call Buddy."

"I'm not going to do anything except look around. If I need help, I'll call you back."

"You won't have time. You're always gettin' in some kinda mess and then—"

"Let's not talk about that on the air," Rhodes said, and signed off. He turned right at the next cross street and headed toward Milsby.

THE MOTORCYCLES SHOT across an intersection a few blocks from where Rhodes was stopped at a stop sign. There were four of them. They had already

turned off the Milsby road and were on the highway
that led out of Clearview toward the southeast. It was
also the highway that led to The County Line, so
Rhodes thought he might as well tag along and see
if that was where they were going.

He was too far away to see who was riding the
motorcycles, but it was reasonable to assume that
Rapper and Nellie were on two of them. There were
very few motorcycles in Blacklin County.

Rhodes stayed far enough behind not to alarm the
bikers. If they were going to The County Line, he
wanted them to get there so he could find out why.
He thought they might be meeting someone.

If they were just leaving Blacklin County for some
reason or other, that was all right, too. He could lo-
cate them eventually if he needed them later on. He
let them pull even farther ahead of him, and soon
they were out of sight.

WHEN HE REACHED The County Line, the parking lot
was not nearly as crowded as it had been the night
before. Sunday night wasn't prime honky-tonking
time in Blacklin County.

That didn't mean there weren't plenty of customers. It just meant that it was easier to park, and that
the early arrivals didn't have to worry about having
their cars blocked in by the latecomers. Rhodes was
able to park much closer to the entrance than he had
done on Saturday. The motorcycles, as usual, were
close to the front. It was a lot easier to maneuver one
of them through the parking lot than it was to maneuver a car.

Now Rhodes had to make a decision. He could go inside and see who Rapper was talking to, if he was talking to anyone besides his pals, or he could wait and see what developed. He decided that he was too impatient to wait, but remembering his comment to Hack about being careful, he thought he'd better call for backup before going inside.

"Buddy's out on a call," Hack said when Rhodes got him. "We got us a four-fifteen at the Dairy Queen."

"Let's switch frequencies," Rhodes said.

Hack agreed, and they changed to a frequency that couldn't be picked up on citizens' scanners.

"Now, what kind of disturbance are they having at the Dairy Queen?" Rhodes asked.

"Fishin'," Hack said.

"Hack…"

"All right. I was just joshin' you a little. But it's the truth. The Methodist preacher's wife took some kids out there to get a Pick-Nic kid's meal after church. You seen the set up they got for those?"

Rhodes had seen it. The kids got to "pick" a prize with their meal, and the local DQ had a display of the prizes in something resembling vending machines.

"You mean Fisher's stuck again?" he said.

"That's right. He didn't learn his lesson like you thought he might. Tried to pick his prize right out of the display. Ran his arm in one of those slots, and it's in there tight as Dick's hat band. I told Buddy to use some of that oil they cook the french fries with on him this time."

"Good idea. What about Ruth?"

"She just checked in. That bullfighter fella is across the line and on his way home."

That meant that Ruth was practically on the other side of the county, but even at that it wouldn't take her long to get to where Rhodes was.

"Send her along for backup," Rhodes said. "You never know what Rapper might do."

"OK. You wait for her to get there before you go in."

"I can't do that. Rapper may be gone by then."

"You never learn, do you?" Hack said.

"Don't worry. I told you I'd be careful."

"Yeah," Hack said. "That's what you always tell me."

THE MUSIC INSIDE The County Line was just as loud as it had been on Saturday, but the crowd on the dance floor was much smaller. There were three bikers drinking beer at the bar, and Rhodes was acquainted with all three of them, though Nellie was the only one whose name he knew. Rapper wasn't there.

Since the three at the bar weren't looking in his direction, Rhodes thought he might as well go have a look at the dancers. Maybe he'd find Rapper dancing with Terry Deedham. That would put an interesting twist on things.

That wasn't what he found. As far as he could tell, Terry wasn't there. There were plenty of blondes, but she wasn't one of them.

Terry's husband was there, however. He was sitting at one of the tables that partially surrounded the dance floor.

And he was talking to Rapper.

Rhodes had seen enough. He knew better than to confront Rapper while his buddies were with him, at least not without backup.

He was about to leave when Rapper looked up and saw him.

FIFTEEN

RAPPER WAS AN OLD HAND at dealing with the law, and the sight of the sheriff didn't visibly affect him. He sat calmly, looking at Rhodes as if they were two old friends who hadn't seen each other in a while.

Everything would have been fine if Rhodes had been dealing only with Rapper. But he wasn't. There was also Deedham to consider, and Deedham, while he might have had nerves of iron when he stalked the sideline of a football field plotting out defenses and revising strategies, had never before been caught in any situation quite as shady as talking to a man like Rapper about whatever it was that they were discussing.

So he panicked.

That wouldn't have been so bad in itself, but in his haste to distance himself from Rapper, Deedham upset the table between them, knocking the two bottles of beer that sat on it into Rapper's lap.

Even that wouldn't have been much of an annoyance in the course of a normal evening at The County Line. Similar things probably happened fairly often, and Rapper took it coolly enough, bending over to pick up the bottles as they slipped from his lap to the floor, the beer puddling around their necks.

What *was* an annoyance, at least to one particular patron of The County Line, was the fact that when

Deedham jumped up, he pushed his chair backward, hard, into the chair of the man at a nearby table.

The man was taking a drink from his beer bottle at the time, and when Deedham's chair hit him, he jammed the bottle into his upper lip, cutting it on his incisors.

The man, having had several earlier beers, wasn't in a mood to be trifled with.

"God damn" he yelled, spinning around and standing up.

Rhodes caught a glimpse of blood on the man's upper lip as he grabbed Deedham by the collar and tried to fling him across the dance floor. The irate customer was much smaller than Deedham and ordinarily wouldn't have been able to fling Deedham very far, but the football coach was off balance and on the run. He stumbled to the dance floor, flapping his arms in an attempt to regain his balance, but he couldn't. He collided with a dancing couple and sent them sprawling. As they fell, they dragged down others, none of whom were pleased with the way things were going.

The man with the bloody lip still wasn't satisfied. He decided that Rapper must have had something to do with things, so he jumped at him across the tipped-over table.

Rapper moved only slightly, and the man went right past him. As he sailed by, Rapper hit him in the back of the head with one of the beer bottles that he had picked up from the floor. The man dropped straight down without making a sound.

He had friends. Three of them. They all jumped

for Rapper, but Rapper had friends too. Attracted by the commotion, they came in from the bar and joined the squabble. Not wanting to be left out, half the people who had been sitting at tables decided to join in as well.

Rhodes tried to get to the dance floor and grab Deedham, but another minor riot had broken out, and he didn't have much luck. No one seemed quite sure who was responsible for knocking everyone down, so to be on the safe side, everyone was trying to take revenge on everyone else.

Women were kicking shins and scratching faces. Men were punching and butting. The County Line's bouncers, two heavily muscled men in tight white T-shirts, had gotten into the action, throwing people aside as they waded through the mob, but they weren't having much effect. Things had gotten out of control too quickly for two men to be able to do anything to quiet people down. Everyone in the place was either yelling or grunting with effort. Rhodes could no longer even hear the music from the jukebox.

Deedham was getting away. He elbowed his way across the dance floor without getting knocked down and reached a door behind the platform where the bands played. A red sign over the door said, FIRE EXIT. A beer bottle aimed at Deedham's head bounced off the protective chicken wire and shattered as it fell.

Rhodes stepped over two men who were wrestling on the floor and shoved aside another man who was staggering around in a stupor. At Rhodes's gentle push, he slid into a silent heap.

"You can't do that to Bo!" a woman screamed.

Rhodes turned his head, and he just had time to read the woman's T-shirt—SEX IS BETTER THAN DRUGS IF YOU HAVE THE RIGHT PUSHER—before she jumped on his back and began to pull his hair.

Rhodes tried to throw her off, but she fastened her left arm around his neck and clamped her skinny legs around his waist. She didn't weigh much, so he kept going.

"You killed Bo!" she yelled, grabbing a handful of hair and yanking.

Rhodes winced, but he didn't bother to tell her that Bo was just drunk. It would have been wasted effort. He carried her past struggling twosomes and three-somes, dodging punches as best he could until he reached the fire exit.

"This is the end of the line, ma'am," he said.

He took her wrist and peeled her arm from around his neck, then grabbed her other wrist and pried her hand loose from his head, losing a little tuft of hair in the process.

He pulled her arms down to his sides, but she refused to release him from her jean-clad legs, clinging to him like some kind of outraged monkey.

He didn't want to hurt her, so he said, "Ma'am, I'm Sheriff Dan Rhodes. If you don't let go of me, I'm going to arrest you for disorderly conduct and assaulting an officer."

"You aren't the sheriff. You killed Bo!"

Rhodes couldn't wait any longer. He didn't want Deedham to get away and do anything foolish.

"I'm sorry I have to do this," he said.

He let go of her right wrist and grabbed her left arm with both hands, giving her what he and all his friends in elementary school had called the Indian Wrist Burn. It was painful but harmless. It was also effective.

The woman screamed and let go with her legs. She sagged to the floor and Rhodes went through the fire exit, leaving her there to rub her arm and wail.

His first thought was that Deedham would try to lose himself in the trees that grew in back of the building, but he saw at once that wasn't a possibility. The trees were too thinly scattered to offer much concealment, and the lights strung in the branches made searching among them too easy. Deedham had gone in another direction.

Rhodes turned to run to the front of the building, which was where Deedham must have parked his car.

By the time he got to the parking lot, the fight had spilled out through the front doors. Brawling was the favorite sport of many of those who frequented The County Line. They were good at it, and they were enthusiastic.

One man had foolishly decided that the bikers were responsible for the whole thing. It was a logical conclusion to draw, considering Rapper's involvement. Logical, but not smart, especially in view of the fact that being unable to find a biker to vent his wrath on, he was taking it out on one of the bikes that he had tipped over. He was holding a bottle of beer and each time he took a sip, he stomped on the spokes of the front wheel with his boot heel.

Even an assault on his person was not as likely to arouse a biker to fury as an attack on his bike, and Rhodes, being too far away to do anything, watched helplessly as Born Too Loose galloped over, grabbed the man by the back of the shirt, turned him around, and hit him in the face five times. When Born Too Loose let the man go, he dropped to the ground and didn't move.

The biker didn't care about the man. He bent over to look at the spokes in the wheel of his bike.

Rhodes looked around for Deedham, but he didn't see him. He did see Rapper, Nellie, and the other biker come out of The County Line. They went straight for their bikes, straddled them, and started the engines. Born Too Loose picked his bike up, shrugged, and cranked it. All four of them turned the bikes to start out of the lot.

While not full, the lot didn't offer a straight line of egress. Rhodes was able to weave through the maze of cars and stand in the bikers' path.

They didn't seem worried by him. Rapper smiled, and his bike jumped forward.

Rhodes stood right in the glare of Rapper's headlight. He pulled his pistol, fired one shot in the air, and leveled the gun at Rapper.

Rapper didn't hesitate. He turned abruptly, his rear tire throwing up a cloud of caliche dust and small stones, most of which ticked off the sides of the cars, all except for the one that bounced off Rhodes's right shoe.

The other bikers, following Rapper's lead, turned as well, heading right back the way they had come.

That was fine with Rhodes. There wasn't any escape for them in that direction.

Or so he'd thought. He hadn't reckoned with the fact that the front door of the honky-tonk was wide open.

Rapper and the others drove straight for it. The fighting stopped as people threw themselves out of the way of the retreating bikers.

Rapper pulled up his front wheel to get it over the single low step, gunned his engine, and shot through the door with the others right behind him. The noise of the bikes' motors thundered through the building.

Rhodes holstered his pistol and ran to the door. He was just in time to see the bikers, Rapper still in the lead, roar across the dance floor, scattering people left and right like terrified chickens.

Rhodes thought the platform would stop them, but he should have known better. Rapper jerked up his front wheel and went airborne, smashing through the chicken-wire-barrier as if it were sewing thread. Rhodes was later sure that he only imagined the twang he heard as the wire broke.

The fire exit door was still open, and Rhodes watched in frustration as the bikers accelerated through it and disappeared, leaving nothing behind but the throbbing echo of their engines.

Rhodes walked over to the bar and leaned against it. Deedham was gone, Rapper was gone, and Rhodes had nothing to show for it.

Zach walked down to him. "You want a Dr. Pepper, Sheriff?"

"I thought you didn't have one."

Zach shrugged. "I don't. I just asked if you wanted one."

"Very funny, Zach. Does this kind of thing happen very often around here?"

Zach looked out over the dance floor, where those customers still standing were helping the others to their feet. Most of them were laughing in spite of bloodied noses, demolished hairdos, torn jeans, and ripped shirts. The bouncers looked as dazed as the customers.

"Now and then," Zach said.

Rhodes could hear the jukebox again, though he couldn't identify the song.

"I saw Bob Deedham in there," he said, nodding toward the dance floor. "He was with a biker named Rapper. Was Rapper the man you saw him with before?"

"I don't know," Zach said. "I didn't see him come in tonight."

Rhodes looked around the room at the people who were coming from the outside.

"I ought to arrest the whole bunch," he said.

"Put quite a strain on the jailhouse if you did," Zach said.

Rhodes pushed away from the bar. He hurt all over, and he was probably going to have more than a few bruises on Monday.

"You're probably right. No wonder we don't get many calls from out here."

"Just doing our civic duty," Zach said. "We wouldn't want to add to the county's problems."

"I appreciate it," Rhodes said, starting for the door.

"And just to show you that there's no hard feelings, I'm not going to bill the county for all the damage you caused, either."

Rhodes turned around. He was still rankled because everyone he'd been after had gotten away.

"Don't push it, Zach."

Zach held up his hands, palms outward. "Just a little joke, Sheriff."

A few people remained out in the parking lot, but they were no longer fighting. Most of them were sitting or leaning on cars, just talking or drinking beer from bottles that they somehow had neither dropped nor spilled during the recent altercation.

Rhodes located his car, got in, and drove away.

HIS MOOD IMPROVED immensely about five miles away from The County Line. That was when he saw Ruth Grady. The bubble bar was flashing on top of her squad car, and she was standing by the door of the car she'd pulled over, shining her flashlight in the face of the driver.

The driver was Bob Deedham.

Rhodes smiled as he pulled over to the shoulder and stopped. He got out and walked up to Ruth.

"Hey, Sheriff," she said. "I was on my out to give you some backup, but this gentleman was headed back to Clearview doing about eighty-five, so

I had to make a U-turn and pull him over. Hope you don't mind."

Rhodes didn't mind at all. "Get out of the car, Deedham. We're going to have to take you in."

Deedham didn't want to get out. "What did I do? You can't take me in for speeding."

"That's true," Rhodes agreed. "We'll take you in for inciting a riot."

"That's not fair! I was just in a hurry to leave. I didn't mean to cause any trouble."

"And there are a few other things, too," Rhodes told him. "Suspicion of murder, for one."

"I didn't kill anybody! What are you talking about?"

"Just get out of the car, Deedham. We'll talk it over at the jail."

Deedham crossed his arms over his chest. "I'm not going anywhere."

Rhodes looked at Ruth. "How long has it been since you shot someone trying to escape?"

"I never did that," Ruth said. She tapped her fingers on the flashlight. "I killed that man last year for speeding to avoid arrest, though. That might work again."

"It would save the state the expense of a trial," Rhodes said. "I'll back you up. You want me to hold the flashlight?"

Ruth handed him the light. "It'll look better if I shoot him through the back glass. You hold that light steady now."

She started to walk to the back of the car.

"You're just trying to scare me," Deedham said. "She won't shoot."

Rhodes took a deep breath. "You're right. I shouldn't joke around like that, but I was still a little upset about what happened back at The County Line. Come on back here, Ruth."

"I sure did want to shoot him, Sheriff," Ruth said when she got back to the door.

"It still might not be a bad idea," Rhodes said. "But that's not the way we work. Look, Deedham, let's put it this way. You're just wanted for questioning. Are you going to come in peacefully?"

"What if I don't?" Deedham asked. "Are you going to shoot me?"

"No," Rhodes said. "I'm sorry about that. I was taking out my frustrations on you, and that wasn't right. On the other hand, I don't like you very much, and if you don't do what I ask you, I'm going to have a little talk with Goober Vance. I'm not going to tell him anything but the truth, and I can't be responsible for what he might put in the paper."

"That son of a bitch," Deedham said.

Rhodes had apparently touched a nerve. "Vance? You have a problem with him?"

"That's my business," Deedham said. He shut his mouth in a tight line.

"Not anymore. It's my business now. And it's going to be the business of everyone in Clearview and all of Blacklin County if Vance prints what I tell him. Are you going to come along or not?"

"I'll come. But I'm not going in any cop car."

"You won't have to. We'll trust you. You can follow Deputy Grady. And I'll be right behind you." Rhodes handed Ruth the flashlight. "Let's go," he said.

SIXTEEN

THE INTERROGATOIN ROOM was as old-fashioned as everything else in the Blacklin County jail. Hack kept saying that someday the county was going to be forced to build a new jail, and then they'd have a proper interrogation room, one with a two-way mirror, a built-in voice-activated recorder, a video camera, and all the other amenities.

That might happen in the unforeseeable future, but for the present they were stuck with an eight-by-ten room with scaly green walls, a scarred wooden table, and three metal folding chairs so old that no one, not even Hack, remembered where they had come from.

"Maybe the old Clippinger funeral home," he had told Rhodes once. "The one Clyde Ballinger bought out. But maybe not. They might be older than that."

No matter how old they were, they were bent and scratched, with legs that were just slightly out of line so that not a single chair sat quite level on the floor.

The floor itself wasn't exactly level, either. It was rough, unfinished concrete, covered with dark stains that Rhodes had never been able to identify, which he figured was just as well, considering what Hack had told him of the history of the room. Rhodes never knew how much of what Hack said was true, though he'd heard similar stories about some of his predecessors for most of his life.

"Old Sheriff Thomason, now," Hack had said, "he was the one that they used to call 'Delco.' That was 'cause he'd take a prisoner in that little back room and whack 'em with a ba'try cable till they told him what he wanted to know. They say he could get a confession out of a man faster than a minnow can swim a dipper.

"That woulda been when you were just a young fella, I guess. Couldn't get away with anything like that these days, even if it did save a lot of hard investigatin'. And before old Delco there was Sheriff Elbert. He's the one liked to use a wet lariat rope. Worked pretty good, from what I hear. Good as a ba'try cable, they say. Yes, sir, that old room's seen a lot of things. Heard 'em, too, I imagine. But I guess I'm just as glad that kinda stuff don't go on these days."

Rhodes, not being a big believer in brutality, was just as glad as Hack was, though there were times when he wondered if maybe Sheriffs Elbert and 'Delco' Thomason didn't have the right idea.

And this was one of those times. Bob Deedham wasn't exactly being cooperative.

Deedham was slumped in one of the rickety chairs, staring at the little tape recorder in the middle of the table. Rhodes was standing across from him, one foot in the seat of a second chair. Ruth was seated in the third chair, watching, listening, and acting as the stenographer, but so far she hadn't had to write down much.

"Look, Deedham," Rhodes said, "We know a lot

already. You might as well go ahead and tell us the rest of it."

"You don't know anything," Deedham said. "You've just been listening to that idiot Goober Vance. If there was ever a guy with the perfect nickname, he's the one. He's the biggest goober in town."

"Goober's not the only one I've talked to," Rhodes said. "But let's just start with him. What's the problem between you two?"

It was obvious to Rhodes there was a problem, and he wanted to find out about it. It might help him to explain why almost all the rumors that Vance had passed along to Rhodes seemed to be extremely exaggerated or to lead nowhere.

"There's not any problem," Deedham said. "You're just fishing."

That reminded Rhodes of something. He turned to Ruth.

"Did Hack say anything to you about the Methodist preacher's son?" he asked.

"He said Buddy got his arm out. The cooking oil worked just fine."

Rhodes nodded and turned back to Deedham. "Now, then. Let's start all over. I didn't just talk to Goober Vance. I talked to some members of the football team who confirmed at least part of what he told me. I've also talked to your wife, and she confirmed the other part. So now it's your turn. If you want to set the record straight, you'd better get started."

Rhodes was exaggerating considerably as far as the confirmations were concerned, but he thought that doing so might give Deedham a push in the right direction.

It did.

"What did Terry say?" Deedham asked. "I'll bet she didn't tell you about Goober Vance trying to put the make on her at The County Line? Did she mention that?"

As a matter of fact, she hadn't mentioned it at all, but that reminded Rhodes of something else. Both Meredith and Roy Kenner had been somewhat more successful with Terry than Vance had. Rhodes wondered whether Terry had ever mentioned them to her husband.

"No, she didn't say anything about Goober. She goes out there to The County Line a lot, doesn't she?"

"I never gave it much thought," Deedham said, which may even have been the truth. Or it may not have been.

"Did she ever talk about any other men? Besides Goober Vance?"

Deedham stiffened. "What's that supposed to mean?"

"Just exactly what it sounds like."

"I know what you're getting at," Deedham said. "I saw her there with Meredith once. Maybe your bartender buddy told you. Well, so what? Terry likes to have a good time, and I'm not much fun for her. She likes dancing, and I like football. If she wants to dance with a guy, I'm not going to try to stop her. She deserves some entertainment."

That was a generous attitude, but considering what

Deedham had told Ruth Grady earlier, Rhodes wasn't convinced that the coach was sincere.

"Why did you lie to Deputy Grady about your wife's relationships with other men?" Rhodes asked.

Deedham looked embarrassed. "It's not the kind of thing you like to admit to anybody, much less to a woman. Besides, I was sure those 'relationships' you're talking about never went beyond The County Line dance floor."

"What if they did?"

Deedham shrugged. "Then they did. I don't think so, though."

Besides, Rhodes thought, deciding that Deedham was being truthful enough, it was football season. Deedham didn't have time to worry much about his wife.

"Your wife enjoys The County Line, but she wasn't there tonight. Why not?"

"She doesn't go on Sunday. She likes to watch '60 Minutes' and 'Murder, She Wrote.'"

"So you knew she wouldn't be there."

"You're getting way off the subject, Sheriff. Don't you want to know about her and Goober Vance?"

"Tell me, then. What *about* her and Goober Vance?"

"That's why that toothpick-chewing son of a bitch is spreading lies about me. He's trying to get back at Terry because she laughed at him when he tried to pick her up. Not that *she'd* tell me that. It was Vance. He was really mad, and he said he'd get me for it. I don't know why he'd want to get me. I didn't do anything."

If Deedham were telling the truth, and Rhodes was beginning to believe more and more that he was, his story might explain a lot. Vance had certainly embellished his account of Terry and Brady Meredith. And he might have been trying to get at her indirectly by implying that someone on the team was considering the use of steroids. Vance had thought Rhodes would be smart enough to know he meant Deedham, but Rhodes had been too intent on Meredith and hadn't caught on.

"So now we know about Vance," Rhodes said. "Let's talk about a man called Rapper."

"I never saw him before," Deedham said too quickly. "He was just some guy I was having a beer with."

"Let's see," Rhodes said. "I believe you were the one who said that, among other things, you didn't like Brady Meredith because he went drinking on the weekends. Do you remember telling me that?"

Deedham admitted that he remembered.

"So tell me where I'm wrong here. This is the weekend. And you were out drinking. You must do it all the time or you wouldn't pick somebody like Rapper to share a table with."

"So I didn't like Meredith. Maybe I don't like myself very much, either."

"Maybe not, but if you don't, it's not because you make a habit of going out to The County Line. I talked to the bartender. You've been there just once before, and you were with Rapper."

"The bartender told you that?"

"Didn't I just say that I talked with the bartender?

He'd make a pretty good witness, too. He's the kind of man who never forgets a face.''

"So you say.''

Deedham was a stubborn cuss. Rhodes wondered if there were any old battery cables lying around the jail. Probably not. So Rhodes would just have to try something else.

"You're right. So I say. And so the bartender will say. And when I tell a representative from the University Interscholastic League that I think you were out there buying steroids, what do you think is going to happen to the Clearview Catamounts?''

Deedham straightened. "Who said anything about steroids?''

"I did.'' Rhodes didn't think it would be wise to mention Goober Vance again. "Rapper is a known drug trafficker, and if any of the Catamounts test positive for drugs, God help you. You'll be begging me to keep you in jail for the rest of your life because you wouldn't dare show your face on the street. You'd be lynched.''

Deedham straightened even more. His chair creaked, and one leg scraped on the concrete floor.

Ruth Grady stood up, holding her steno pad. "Don't be too hard on him, Sheriff. Maybe he was just trying to help the team.''

"Steroids don't help anyone,'' Rhodes said. "And they're illegal. Clearview will have to forfeit every single game of the season.''

"Maybe we can find a way around that,'' Ruth said. She walked over to stand by Deedham. "We can't let a man's reputation go down the drain if he was just trying to help.''

Rhodes thought she was overdoing the Good Cop bit a little. He said, "I don't see how. Cheating is cheating. Breaking the law is breaking the law.''

"I didn't break the law," Deedham said. He slumped back down in the chair. "I tried, but I didn't do it.''

Now they were getting somewhere, Rhodes thought. He said, "Tell us about it.''

Deedham did. He'd found out about Rapper through a sporting-goods salesman. He refused to name the salesman, but Rhodes wasn't interested in that right now. He could find out later. He told Deedham to go on.

Deedham explained that the salesman had set it up for Rapper and Deedham to meet. Deedham had picked the spot. He didn't think anyone would find it curious if a coach had a drink with a biker. They'd just be two guys who met at a bar.

"But he never sold me any drugs. I'd decided by the first time I talked to him that I didn't want to risk it. We'd worked too hard this season to take the chance of losing everything because of something that I'd done.''

Rhodes could see where Deedham might have been of two minds about things. The team was winning without the drugs, and winning was all Deedham cared about. As long as they were winning, there was no need to take the risk.

"Besides,'' Deedham went on, "I'd sort of hinted

around to some of the team, and it was pretty obvious that they weren't interested.''

"Brady Meredith," Rhodes said. "He preached against drugs pretty hard."

"He sure did, and he was right. I'm sorry I ever got mixed up in anything like that. I shouldn't have let wanting to win get to me like it did.''

"If you're so sorry, what were you doing out at The County Line tonight?" Rhodes asked.

Deedham shook his head wearily. "I was stupid. Just talking to Rapper in the first place was stupid. I thought it didn't matter how you won, just as long as you won. Surely you've seen how much winning the district means to everybody in Clearview. But if you get involved with the wrong people, it makes a difference. It takes away from the winning. I should have known better.''

Everything that Deedham said was true, but Rhodes didn't want to appear to be sympathizing with him.

"You were stupid, all right," he said. "You didn't just talk to him once. You went back.''

"Because he threatened me," Deedham said. "He said he thought we had an agreement. He said he'd taken a risk for me, and that I was going to have to pay off or he'd tell about the steroids.''

"Who was he going to tell?" Rhodes asked. "Meredith?"

"Brady was already dead when Rapper called me. He was going to tell Jasper if I didn't buy the drugs.''

"Jasper wouldn't have liked that," Rhodes said.

Deedham looked up. "Wouldn't have liked it?

He'd have killed me.'' Deedham thought about what he'd just said. "Well, he wouldn't have done that, but he would've fired me, and he would've put out the word on me. I wouldn't have been able to get another job in this state, not in coaching.''

"So what were you going to do about it?''

"I was going to pay Rapper off,'' Deedham said. "I was just going to give him the money and not take the drugs. He said that would be fine. The money was all he wanted, something to compensate him for his trouble. We were just about to settle up when you walked in.''

Everything that Deedham said made sense, and it sounded a lot like the truth. But that still didn't let Deedham off the hook for Brady Meredith's murder. Rhodes thought it was time to move on to that.

"Do you smoke, Deedham?'' he asked.

"No. Why?''

"No reason. Did you see Meredith after the game Friday night?''

"Wait a minute. Why are you asking me that? I've already told your deputy about that.''

"You lied to her about your wife. Maybe you lied about that, too.''

Deedham looked for a second as if he might stand up. Rhodes put the foot that was in the chair down on the floor and braced himself.

Ruth started her Good Cop act again. "The sheriff has to go over some of the same ground I covered,'' she said. "It doesn't mean that he suspects you of anything.''

"*Do* you suspect me?'' Deedham asked Rhodes.

"Just answer the question," Rhodes told him. "Did you see Meredith after the game?"

Deedham looked at the tape recorder as if to check on whether it was still working. It was.

"I saw him. So did Jasper and Kenner. We were in the locker room with the team. For that matter, so was Goober Vance, the son of a bitch who's trying to set me up. He knows that if we lose to Springville, it'll kill me. He's trying to keep me distracted."

"Vance isn't trying to set you up," Rhodes said, wondering if Deedham connected everything in his life to football. "You've done a pretty good job of that all by yourself. Dealing with Rapper was stupid; you said so yourself. And you said something else. You said that Jasper would kill you if he found out you were messing around and trying to make a drug buy."

"That's right, but I didn't really mean that."

"What would Brady Meredith have done if he'd found out?"

Deedham opened his mouth, but no words came out.

"And more to the point," Rhodes said, "what would you have done to protect yourself from him if he'd found out?"

This time Deedham was able to answer. "I didn't kill Brady. Why can't you believe that?"

"Because you haven't convinced me."

"Then maybe I need a lawyer. Maybe I'd better just shut up."

"You don't need a lawyer," Ruth said. "The sheriff has to ask you these questions, but that doesn't mean he really thinks you did it. You haven't been formally charged with anything, and you can leave any time.''

Deedham seemed to relax a little, but not much. "Just the same, I don't think I want to answer any more questions.''

"You should," Ruth said. "You'll just make yourself look guilty if you don't.''

Deedham thought about it. "All right. But I don't see why you can't just believe me.''

"We're not in the believing business right now," Rhodes said. "How long did you stay at the field house after the game?''

"Late. Just like I told your deputy. Everyone else had been gone for a good while by the time I got through with the films. And Terry was asleep when I got home. I didn't kill Brady. Studying those films is more important to me than anything else. I was there, all right.''

"What was Goober Vance doing in the locker room?''

"He's always there after the game, getting quotes from the team and the coaches to use in those idiotic articles he writes. Do you ever read them?''

"Sometimes," Rhodes said.

"Then you know what I mean. Say, wait a minute. Maybe he killed Brady.''

"Why would he do that?" Rhodes asked.

"You'd have to ask him about that. He didn't like Brady much more than he liked me, though. He never said anything about it, but you could tell.''

"How?"

"The way he looked at him when he thought Brady couldn't see him. He didn't like him a damn bit. I'd talk to him if I were you."

Rhodes said he'd be sure to do that. Then he asked Deedham about Hayes Ford.

"That bookie? I know who he is, but I don't know him. What's he got to do with all this?"

Rhodes wondered how much he should tell Deedham. He didn't want to give away too much, but at the same time he had to keep the coach talking.

"I saw someone talking to him before the game Friday night. I think it might have been Brady Meredith."

"Jesus," Deedham said. "Brady wasn't that dumb, was he?"

"You tell me," Rhodes said.

Deedham looked at the scaly green wall, then up at Rhodes. "That would be dumber than steroids. We'd forfeit everything if Brady was betting on the games."

Rhodes decided to let Deedham know a little more about his thinking on the subject. "What if Brady was shaving points?"

"Are you kidding me?"

"It's just a thought," Rhodes said.

"Well, you can forget it."

Deedham closed his mouth in a tight line and sat silently. Rhodes sat down and watched him. The room grew uncomfortably quiet.

After several minutes had passed, Deedham said,

"You know something, Sheriff? You might be right."

"About the points?"

"If you think about what happened at the game, it could look that way. And there were a couple of other things earlier in the season."

"The Westico game," Rhodes said.

Deedham looked surprised. "That's right. And the one with Fondrell."

"But you didn't know about any connection between Brady and Hayes Ford?"

"No. And it's hard to believe that he'd be talking to him before the game." Deedham thought for a while. "But come to think of it, he disappeared from the sidelines while the team was going through its pre-game drill. He showed up again just in time for the school song."

That fit with what Rhodes had observed in the stadium parking lot before the game. Brady, if it had been Brady talking to Ford, hadn't really been taking much of a risk. Most everyone arrived for the game on time. As Rhodes recalled, there had been no one else around, and it was dark. He had noticed the two men himself only by accident.

"Someone killed Ford earlier today," Rhodes said.

Deedham's jaw dropped. "You don't think it was me, do you?"

"I hope not," Rhodes told him.

SEVENTEEN

"SO YOU JUST LET HIM GO?" Ivy asked.

She and Rhodes were sitting on the living-room couch, watching a late movie on one of the cable channels. It was *Across the Wide Missouri*, with Clark Gable and Ricardo Montalban, who was playing an Indian. Rhodes had seen it before. As he recalled, Gable was eventually going to run out of ammunition for his cap-and-ball rifle, but being a clever frontier type, old Clark would fire the rifle with the ramrod in its barrel, sending it to pierce Montalban's chest.

"I let him go," Rhodes confirmed. "There wasn't enough evidence to charge him with anything, and I really don't think he did it. He was too convincing."

Rhodes took a handful of popcorn from the bowl on the coffee table. It was air-popped, with no butter or salt, and it was about like eating the Styrofoam peanuts that shippers used for packing. Rhodes preferred his popcorn greasy and salty, although he supposed the plain stuff was better than nothing. But not much better.

"What about Rapper?" Ivy asked.

Ivy had met Rapper on the biker's previous visit to Blacklin County. She knew enough about him to know he was capable of murder.

"Rapper's a diffcrent story," Rhodes said. "But

maybe his involvement didn't go any farther than trying to sell steroids to Deedham.''

"Do you really believe that?''

"I'm not sure. There's one thing on his side, though, and if I could talk to him, I might be able to clear things up.''

"I can't think of a single good thing about that man. Tell me what's on his side.''

Rhodes was tired of Gable. He reached for the remote and changed the channel. He bypassed the woman selling cubic zirconia earrings and the man selling exercise equipment. He stopped on a channel where Ghidorah, the three-headed monster, was flapping around on the ground, battling it out with Rodan, Godzilla, and Mothra. There was a huge dust cloud forming around all the rubber monsters. Rhodes smiled. That was more like it. He reached for another handful of popcorn.

"I don't see how you can watch that stuff,'' Ivy said.

Rhodes had to admit that it wasn't exactly Art. Not only that, it was probably the direct ancestor of a show like the "Mighty Morphin Power Rangers," and Rhodes didn't understand how anyone could watch *that*.

"I don't either,'' he said. "I just sort of like it.''

"To each his own. What about Rapper?''

"Well, the first time I talked to him, when I got into that little scuffle with Nellie, I gave him a chance to get out of the county, just pack up his tent and go. He didn't like the idea. In fact, he's still around. I think that if he'd killed Meredith, he'd have left without much of an argument. Why take the chance of getting mixed up in a murder again?"

"He got away with it once," Ivy said.

"He was lucky, and he knows it. All he lost was part of a few fingers. But he wouldn't be that lucky again, and he surely wouldn't make it so easy for me to find him by hanging around places like The County Line."

"So you think he was just after the money that he thought Bob Deedham owed him?"

"That's what I think now, but I could be wrong. I'm not crossing him off my list."

"Who else is on that list?"

"Well, there's Deedham, for one. I don't think he did it, but I'm not absolutely certain. And then there's Goober Vance. I just added him."

"What about Terry Deedham and Nancy Meredith? I thought that when a man was murdered, you always suspected the wife and the girlfriend."

"I do. But there's a problem with suspecting them. To tell you the truth, there's a problem with all of them."

"What's the problem?"

"I can't tie any of them to Hayes Ford, and I'm certain that the two murders are connected. So what did any of my suspects have to do with Ford?"

On the TV screen, the monsters were now crushing cardboard buildings that were apparently supposed to represent Tokyo, a city that Rhodes figured must have been wiped out by movie monsters about a hundred times. The celluloid citizens must have gotten pretty tired of rebuilding.

Ivy had a suggestion about how to tie one of the suspects in Meredith's death to Hayes Ford. "Nancy Meredith might have wanted to get rid of Ford to save her husband's reputation."

"That would explain the stolen records, all right," Rhodes admitted. "But why would she kill Brady?"

"Hey, I can't do *all* the work for you," Ivy said. "The popcorn bowl's empty, and you've probably seen this movie three times. Don't you think it's about time for bed?"

Rhodes said that he guessed so, but what with one thing and another it was a long time before he got to sleep. Just as he was about to drift off, he heard Speedo barking, and then, he thought, the sound of motorcycles, dim and far away.

THE NEXT MORNING Rhodes was up and out on the job early. Hack had called to say that there was going to be trouble because J. D. Spence was on his way to town.

J.D. was somewhere in the neighborhood of ninety-five years old. No one knew exactly how old he was because J.D. had never said. He'd been in an automobile accident about five years previously. It hadn't amounted to much, just a bent fender, but Rhodes had discovered that J.D. had no driver's license. There was no way the old man could have passed the test to get one. His eyesight was poor because of his cataracts, and his coordination was worse than his eyesight, so Rhodes had forbidden him to drive.

Spence had defied the prohibition, driving to town

a couple of times in his 1963 Ford Falcon, and Rhodes had been forced to ticket him. Since then Spence, who lived about two miles outside of Clearview, had taken to coming into town on his old riding lawn mower.

"Ms. Hatley phoned to warn us," Hack told Rhodes. "She went out to get her paper and saw Mr. Spence rattlin' down the county road stirrin' up the dust. You might wanta drive out that way and see if you can get him turned around."

There wasn't any law that Rhodes could find that would keep a man from riding his lawn mower to town. You didn't need a license to drive one.

The trouble was that when he got to town, Mr. Spence got in the way of the regular traffic. And he didn't always bother to follow the traffic laws. More than once, he'd driven right up on the sidewalk and practically mowed down the pedestrians. The noise from the mower's clattery old engine frightened any children who happened to be around, and once Mr. Spence had driven right through the big double doors at the H.E.B. Rhodes had caught up with him in the produce department.

As soon as Rhodes turned off the blacktop onto the gravel, he saw Mr. Spence coming. He pulled over to the side of the road to wait for the approaching lawn mower, parking with two wheels on the gravel and two on the slanting shoulder. He rolled down the window and made himself comfortable.

After a couple of minutes, Mr. Spence chugged up beside him, stopped, and cut the lawn mower's engine. Spence had once been a sizable man, but old age had shriveled him. His skin was wrinkled and loose, and his eyes were a pale, faded blue. He had on a sweat-stained gray felt hat, a plaid shirt, and a worn pair of black corduroy pants.

"Heighdy, Sheriff," he said. "Looks like it's gonna be a nice day."

Rhodes agreed. There were only a few scraps of cloud in the sky, and the temperature was already into the fifties.

"I got a little touch of the arthuritis, though," Spence said.

Rhodes said that maybe the sun would help.

"Might. Might not. Anyway, I'm glad I run into you. I was comin' into town to see you about a couple of things."

"What things?" Rhodes asked.

"One thing's that injunction or whatever you call it that those Garton sonsabitches 're filin' against our boys. I heard about it on the radio first thing this mornin', and I knew I had to come into town and find out about it."

"Do you follow the games?" Rhodes asked.

"Hell, yes. I been followin' the games ever since I was just a kid myself. I used to be in the grandstand ever' Friday night, and when I couldn't be there or the games was out of town, I'd listen on the radio. All I can do now is listen on the radio, though, since *somebody* won't let me drive to town anymore."

He gave Rhodes a hard look, squinting his watery eyes under his hat brim.

"That injunction's not going to amount to anything," Rhodes said. "No judge is going to overrule an official that was right there on the field."

"I didn't think so," Mr. Spence said. "But these days you never can tell. Too many lawyers is what I say. Anyway, I sure wish I could've seen that game. It must've been somethin'. But a fella that can't drive can't go to the games."

"I'm sure you could find someone to take you to the home games," Rhodes said. "And if you can't, I can. If you want me to, I'll ask around."

"Now that'd be real nice of you. 'Specially since you're the one won't let me drive. I'd'a never thought that Will-o'-the-Wisp Dan Rhodes would've kept an old man away from the football games."

Rhodes was a little embarrassed that Mr. Spence remembered his one moment of fame. To change the subject he said, "What was the other thing you wanted to see me about?"

"Other thing?"

Mr. Spence looked vague. He took off his hat and wiped his hand across the top of his bald head. He put the hat back on, pressing it down so that it mashed down on the tops of his ears, making them stick out at a funny angle.

"You said you wanted to see me about a couple of things," Rhodes told him. "One was the injunction. What was the other one?"

"Oh, yeah."

Mr. Spence smiled broadly. He still had a great many of his teeth, but there didn't seem to be any two of them together, giving his smile a snaggle-toothed charm.

"The other thing was somethin' that woke me up last night," he said.

"And what was that?" Rhodes asked.

Mr. Spence smiled again. "Motorsickles," he said.

RHODES DROVE about a hundred yards past Mr. Spence's house and turned down a one-lane dirt road that was lined with leafless trees. Their branches reached out and almost scraped the county car, and Rhodes wondered if the treewhacker would be coming down that way in the spring. It did a good job of cutting back the limbs that stretched toward passing cars, but Rhodes wasn't fond of the treewhacker, having come a little too close to getting whacked by it himself at one time. He'd just as soon not see it again.

According to Mr. Spence, the narrow, tree-lined road led to an abandoned house that had just about fallen to pieces.

"But the barn's in pretty good shape," Mr. Spence said. "The folks who owned the place, the Pearsons they was, I think, they didn't put much stock in takin' care of their house, but they did just fine on the barn."

Rhodes and Mr. Spence both figured that the motorcycles meant someone might be using the barn to bunk in.

"Why else would anybody be ridin' out here on motorsickles?" Mr. Spence asked. "Ain't another damn thing around here for miles, that I can see."

Mr. Spence hadn't actually visited the barn in several years, but he thought it would provide a decent shelter.

"That is, it would if you don't mind mice. Never knew an old barn that didn't have mice in it. And where there's mice, there's gonna be them damn hognose snakes. I never did like a snake, not even a hognose snake, even if they do eat mice. But there prob'ly won't be no snakes this time of the year, bein's how it's gettin' on toward winter. So I guess it'll be just mice. Mice like to come inside where it's warm, just like people do."

Rhodes didn't think Rapper and his friends would mind mice. He made Mr. Spence promise to turn his lawn mower around and go home, and then he headed for the Pearson place.

The house was just about as Mr. Spence had described it. The porch was still intact, though it had sagged in the middle. The faded walls of the house were intact as well, but they too had sagged inward when the roof collapsed. Dull-red bricks from the chimney littered the ground on one side.

The barn was about fifty yards behind what was left of the house. Probably the reason it was still standing was that it had been built of sheet iron that was now covered with the gritty reddish-brown rust of age.

The barn had a covered feeding area, but the wooden feeding trough that had once been there was long gone. One of the support posts was missing, and the roof sagged down at one end. At the other end of the barn there was a large storage room that Rhodes knew would have a wooden floor built well up off the ground. That was where the mice would be, if there were any mice. That was also where Rapper and his friends would be staying.

Rhodes knew Rapper was there, and probably Nellie as well. He could see two motorcycles parked under the overhang where the feeding trough had once been, and while he was far from an expert, the motorcycles looked to him like the same ones Nellie and Rapper had been riding at the Gottschalk farm. Born Too Loose and his pal must have left the county, or at least Rhodes hoped they had.

Rhodes parked his car in front of the house where it couldn't be seen from the barn and radioed Hack.

"Has Ruth checked in this morning?" he asked.

"She's right here. You want to talk to her?"

"No need for that. You know where the old Pearson place is, around the corner from where J. D. Spence lives?"

"I guess I know where just about ever' place in this county is. Why?"

"There's somebody staying there. I want you to send Ruth out here. I might need some backup."

"I'm surprised you'd ask. And this is the second time lately. You must be gettin' smarter in your old age."

"You can skip the editorial comment," Rhodes said, and signed off.

RHODES KNEW that the smart thing to do would be to wait until Ruth arrived. Or then again, that might *not* be the smart thing to do. Rhodes looked at his watch. It was seven-thirty. Right now there didn't seem to be any sign of activity at the barn, but before too long Rapper or Nellie or both of them would be stirring around. It might be a good idea to tackle them before they had a chance to come to full alertness. If he waited too long, they might even decide to leave.

It wouldn't hurt to walk down to the barn and have a look at things, he told himself. He would be very quiet. Rapper and Nellie were probably still asleep. He could wake them and arrest them without a struggle.

He was almost to the barn when the outside door of the storage room opened and Nellie stepped out. He saw Rhodes immediately and did an almost comical double take before he popped right back through the door that remained open, dangling on its sprung hinges.

Bad idea, Rhodes thought. I'm not as smart as Hack thinks I am. I should have stayed in the car.

But it was too late to worry about having lost the element of surprise. Rhodes drew his sidearm and walked steadily toward the door.

He was still twenty yards away when he heard a loud slam. There was another door, this one leading to the feeding area. Nellie and Rapper both piled out, jumped on their bikes, and kicked them into life. The rumble of the engines reverberated off the sheet iron.

The bikes roared out of the feeding area, with dirt spurting from beneath their back wheels and headed straight for Rhodes. It was obvious that this time Rapper wasn't going to turn back as he had at The

County Line. He was going to run Rhodes down and flatten him into the pasture grass.

Rhodes didn't bother to fire a warning shot.

He aimed at Rapper and pulled the trigger.

EIGHTEEN

RHODES DIDN'T SHOOT to kill. He just wanted to slow Rapper down or throw him off course.

The bullet pinged off the motorcycle's gas tank and sliced through the leg of Rapper's pants. It didn't do a thing to slow the biker down, and it didn't cause him to alter his course by a millimeter. Rhodes barely had time to jump to one side and avoid being flattened.

Rapper stuck out his leg as he sped past and kicked hard at Rhodes. He hit the sheriff's gun hand with the steel toe of his black leather boot, and Rhodes's pistol went spinning away.

Rhodes didn't have a chance to go after it. He had to dive to his left to avoid Nellie, who was thundering along in his pal's wake.

Rhodes landed on his stomach and rolled across the dead grass. He felt his new glasses break.

Oh, well, he thought. At least no one had kept any cattle on the Pearson place for the last few years.

He didn't have time to be grateful for long, however, because Rapper and Nellie were coming back after him.

Rhodes experienced a strong feeling of déjà vu, remembering the last time he and Rapper had tangled and Rapper had lost part of his fingers.

Rapper might have been remembering the same

thing. Rhodes could see that he was smiling, maybe because this time Rhodes didn't have a hoe handle.

Rhodes didn't have his pistol, either, and he couldn't see where it had gone.

There was only one thing to do in that case, and Rhodes did it. He turned and ran for the barn, wishing that he was still the Will-o'-the-Wisp.

He wasn't, but the two bikes roaring along at his back gave the incentive he needed to run as fast as he was capable of, which wasn't very. At least he had a head start, even if it wasn't much of one. As he labored ungracefully across the grass, he imagined he could feel the treads of Rapper's front tire running up his back.

Rapper was yelling something at either Rhodes or Nellie, but Rhodes couldn't make out what it was because his blood was pounding too loudly in his ears. He couldn't even hear the roar of the motorcycles behind him, and he didn't dare look back to see how close they were. He kept his eyes focused on the barn door.

It was only about ten yards away, and Rhodes covered those yards in what seemed like one giant step, throwing himself toward the open door as if he were straining for the end zone in the championship game.

He flew through the opening and hit the wooden floor just as Rapper swooshed by, skidding into an odorous bedroll that belonged to either Rapper or Nellie. There had been hay stored in the barn at one time, and though that had been long ago and virtually nothing remained of it, Rhodes could smell it in the dust that rose from the floor. Even the smell of the bedroll couldn't mask it.

Rhodes sat up, looking around the storage room for anything that could be used as a weapon. Rapper and Nellie hadn't left him much that he could see, and he was about to search through their gear when he saw something hanging from a nail on one of the bare studs. It was a hay hook.

The hook was attached to a short wooden handle and looked like it belonged at the end of a pirate's hand. Rhodes walked over and took it down, fitting his own hand around the smoothly worn handle. Rhode's hand was throbbing, and a bruise was forming on his wrist where Rapper had kicked him, but he could grip the handle easily. The hook wouldn't be good for anything other than close-in work, but it was better than nothing. It was too bad there wasn't a pitchfork.

Rhodes heard someone yelling outside. It was Nellie, who said, "I've got his pistol, Rapper."

That wasn't exactly good news, and neither was Rapper's reply.

"Well, use it then."

Rhodes didn't really expect Nellie to start shooting. Both he and Rapper would have known that if they killed a law officer, even Texas wouldn't be big enough to hide in.

Apparently they didn't care. Maybe it was the excitement of the moment, or maybe they were just crazy. Or maybe they were the ones who had killed Brady Meredith and thought that another murder wouldn't really make much difference.

Rhodes heard the sharp report of the pistol, and a bullet spanged through the sheet-metal wall about three feet to his right.

The bullet went right on out through the other wall, and Rhodes hit the floor.

Nellie fired three more times in rapid succession, but none of the bullets came anywhere near Rhodes, who could see the dust motes dancing in the sunlight that slanted in through the bullet holes. The dust made him sneeze. He had always been allergic to hay.

"Think I got him?" Nellie called out.

"Why don't you go in and see?" Rapper suggested.

That was Rapper, Rhodes thought. Always considerate of his friends.

But Nellie wasn't entirely stupid. "You go," he said. "You're closer than I am."

Rhodes didn't care which of them came, and he didn't care if neither of them did. He was going to stay right where he was until Ruth arrived. He was sure that she'd be there soon.

He heard a motorcycle getting closer, and he rolled to the right of the door and stood up quietly. The sound of the bullets whanging through the metal walls was still ringing in his ears, but he thought he could hear mice chittering under the floor. They were probably more frightened than Rhodes was.

"Can you see him?" Nellie called.

"It's dark in there," Rapper said.

He was only a few feet from where Rhodes stood,

and Rhodes tightened his grip on the hay hook. His wrist gave a little twinge, but he ignored it.

"Can you hear anything?" Nellie asked.

"Not with you yelling like that," Rapper answered.

"Better get off your bike and check it out. See if he's playin' 'possum."

"Why should I check it out? I didn't leave anything in that barn that I have to have. If he's dead, he's dead; if he's not, to hell with him. Let's just ride on out of here and not come back."

Apparently Rapper's desire for revenge had played out. Either that or he had realized how stupid he and Nellie were being.

"Fine with me," Nellie said. "I never did like the idea of coming back to this county in the first place."

It might have been fine with Nellie for them to leave, but it wasn't fine with Rhodes. He couldn't let them go. They might be able to elude the law for a long time if they did. He peeped through one of the bullet holes to see where Rapper was located and saw the biker straddling his machine right in front of the doorway.

Rhodes gathered himself and whirled through the door, making a jump for Rapper. He saw Rapper's eyes widen in surprise, and then he crashed into him, dragging him off the bike, and rolled away. Rapper got to his feet first and charged Rhodes, who had somehow managed to hang onto the hay hook without puncturing some tender part of his anatomy.

Rhodes rose to his knees and swung the hook just before Rapper reached him. The hook hit Rapper's upper thigh with a sound that was solid and meaty and wet all at the same time, and Rhodes jerked backward.

Rapper's leg slipped out from under him, and his foot barely missed Rhodes's head. Rapper screamed and collapsed in a heap, writhing on the ground in front of Rhodes, his hands clutching at the hook sunk into his leg.

Nellie, with a show of disloyalty that didn't surprise Rhodes in the least, turned his bike for the road and roared away.

He didn't get far. Ruth Grady was just pulling into the yard, and she spun the steering wheel, positioning her car to block the gate.

Nellie veered off the path and tried to jump the sagging barbed wire fence, but the bike didn't make it. The front wheel caught the top wire, which stretched a little but didn't break. Nellie's bike flipped over twice before it landed in the middle of the dirt road.

By the time the motorcycle hit the ground, Nellie was no longer on it. He landed six feet away, right beside J. D. Spence, who had followed Ruth on his riding mower.

Spence looked down into Nellie's face and said, "Who the hell are you?"

Nellie didn't even open his eyes. He just groaned.

BOTH RAPPER AND NELLIE wound up in the Clearview General Hospital. Nellie had a couple of broken ribs, and the hay hook had done something to one of the major muscles in Rapper's thigh. The doctor wasn't sure just what without doing a more complete examination, though he thought it was a serious tear, and he was afraid that Rapper would have a little trouble walking for a while. Maybe permanently.

"Reckon he's gonna sue us for police brutality?" Hack wondered. "It wouldn't be the first time you've got sued."

"I don't think he'll bother," Rhodes said. "But maybe this time he's learned his lesson."

Rhodes had gone by the jail after leaving his prisoners at the hospital. He needed to check on what other things might be going on in town. It appeared that nothing much was happening. Monday was usually a quiet day, and Ruth and Buddy had things under control.

"If he ain't learned his lesson this time, he never will," Lawton said. "Lost some fingers the first time, gonna be walkin' with a limp this time. Only way it could've been better is if there was a barb on that hook. They would've had a heck of a time gettin' it out of him, messed up the muscle even worse than it did. If he ever comes back here, Lord knows what'll happen to him. He'll prob'ly get killed."

"I doubt it," Rhodes said. "People like Rapper never die. They just keep on causing trouble."

"Do you think he's the one killed Brady Meredith?" Hack asked.

"There's no evidence pointing that way," Rhodes said.

After the ambulance came to take Nellie and Rapper to town, Rhodes and Ruth had searched the barn. They had found no trace of the drugs that Bob Deed ham was supposed to pay for, and Rhodes was sure that Rapper had sent them out of the county with the other two bikers.

A pistol had been stuck deep in one of the bedrolls, but it was a Glock 9mm, certainly not the weapon used to kill Meredith. Rhodes was just as glad he hadn't found it when he was looking for something to use against Rapper and Nellie. He might have been tempted to shoot one or both of them, and their injuries might have been even worse than they were.

Unlike their last experience in Blacklin County, this time both Nellie and Rapper were guaranteed to spend some time in jail. Rhodes was still adding up the charges against them, but there would be enough to ensure that neither man would get away with serving his entire sentence in the hospital.

The bad news was that actual sentences didn't have much to do with the time served. Because of the crowded prisons, inmates in Texas were currently serving about a month for each year of their sentence before being released. Unless Rapper and Nellie were guilty of one or both of the murders that Rhodes was trying to solve, they would be back in the saddles of their motorcycles in months rather than years. If they were the ones who had murdered Brady Meredith, they'd still get out in a much shorter time than they deserved.

Rhodes didn't let things like that bother him, however. His job was to enforce the law to the best of his ability. What happened to the bad guys after they passed through his hands wasn't up to him, and a few months of jail time were better than no jail time at all.

"Where you gonna be the rest of the day?" Hack asked. "In case I get any more people makin' irate calls about you ruinin' the football season for ever'body, I might wanta sic 'em onto you."

"You didn't mention any irate calls," Rhodes said.

"Well, that don't mean there ain't been any."

"Folks think it's all your fault," Lawton said. "Specially since the word's got out about Hayes Ford. What they're sayin' is that—"

"Wait a minute," Rhodes said, interrupting him. "What's all my fault?"

'Gettin' the team all in an uproar," Lawton said. "See, folks think that—"

This time, Hack interrupted him. "I'm the one that's been takin' the calls. Seems like I oughta be the one to tell the sheriff about 'em."

"Go ahead then," Lawton said, crossing his arms on his chest. "I'm just the one that saved the whole team from gettin' kicked out of the play-offs by drivin' that ambulance on the field and stoppin' the riot. But that's all right. Never mind about me."

"We won't," Hack said, not even looking at him. "Anyhow, the talk is that Hayes Ford gettin' killed like that must have somethin' to do with Brady Meredith. And if the team was upset before, they're really gonna be worried now. If you'd done somethin' about Brady before now, Hayes would still be alive, and then things would all be just fine."

"So what're you gonna do about it?" Lawton said

when Hack paused for breath. He got a quick glare from Hack, but that was all.

"I guess I'll go talk to Goober Vance," Rhodes said. "Maybe he knows something. Maybe he'll even confess."

"Try to make him do it in time to get it in today's paper," Hack said. "Maybe Goober could write it up himself."

"That'd be a first," Lawton said. "Reporter admits he's guilty of murder and writes up his confession for the paper. Might make a good Movie of the Week."

"If he confesses, it might," Hack said. "If he don't, what're we gonna do for an endin'?"

"Big fight in the pressroom," Lawton said. "Sheriff knocks him around for a while and then it winds up with them big rollers where they print the paper up. He slides out on page one, flat as a flitter, and they have to scrape him up off the floor with a spatch'la."

"I don't think they print papers up like that anymore," Hack said. "Not with them big rollers."

"What do you know about how they print up newspapers?" Lawton asked.

"I know as much as you do, that's how much."

"Who says?"

"I say. What is it makes you think you know anything about it anyway?"

When Rhodes slipped out the door, they were still arguing about it.

NINETEEN

GOOBER WASN'T at the newspaper offices. He was "on assignment."

"That's what he always tells us to say," the secretary told Rhodes. "What it means is that he's gone to eat at the Dairy Queen. This is Bean Day. Goober never misses Bean Day."

For reasons that Rhodes had yet to determine, since beans seemed to have very little to do with soft ice cream, the manager of the Clearview Dairy Queen had declared that every Monday would be Bean Day.

The manager, Gene Jackson, went in early, before sunup, and started a huge pot of pinto beans cooking on the stove. When the cook came in, she made cornbread instead of hamburgers, and most everyone who ate lunch at the Dairy Queen that day had the special: all the pinto beans and cornbread you could eat for a dollar and a half.

Rhodes had to admit that it was a good deal. It was cheap, it was filling, and it was low in fat, especially if you could resist getting a Heath Bar Blizzard afterward.

Considering how many lunches he'd missed lately, Rhodes thought it would be a good idea to have some beans and then talk to Vance at the Dairy Queen if they could find a booth with a little privacy.

Rhodes should have known better. Bean Day was something of a phenomenon, fast on its way to becoming a cherished local tradition. The parking lot was jammed, and there was hardly a vacant seat in the place.

Goober Vance was sitting in a booth back near the restrooms. Ron Tandy and Clyde Ballinger were with him. Rhodes helped himself to a bowl of beans and got a slice of cornbread. There were two kinds, regular and jalapeño. Rhodes took a piece of the jalapeño and went toward the rear booth.

Several people stopped him to say hello and to ask what progress he was making on his investigations. None of them seemed irate, for which Rhodes was grateful.

He gave all of them the same answer: "We're doing what we can."

And they all told him practically the same thing: "I sure hope you can get it taken care of before it affects the team too much."

When Rhodes arrived at the back booth, Ron Tandy moved over to make room for him.

"I didn't think you were a bean man," Tandy said.

"Only on Mondays," Rhodes said, sitting down.

"Want some black pepper?" Ballinger asked, offering Rhodes a couple of white paper packets. "Gene never uses enough black pepper."

Rhodes waved the packets aside. He didn't need black pepper; he had the jalapeño cornbread.

"What about this Hayes Ford deal?" Vance said.

"Do you have anything you can say on the record for me?"

"You probably know more than I do," Rhodes told him, wondering if Vance would see a double meaning in the statement.

If he did, he didn't show it. "I don't know a thing other than what I was able to get out of your dispatcher when I called. I thought I might hear something about a big loser in some card game, but there's no word out on the streets about what happened."

Rhodes took a spoonful of beans to keep from smiling. Talking about the "word on the streets" in Clearview was just short of ludicrous. Vance seemed constitutionally unable to avoid a cliché when he had a chance to use one.

"I've heard a few things," Tandy said. "I've heard that Ford's murder has something to do with Brady's. If that's true, it's going to have a bad effect on the team."

There it was again. The message was clear, just as it had been in the phone calls that Hack had gotten, just as it had been from practically everyone Rhodes had talked to. No one really seemed to care about Ford, any more than they seemed to care about Brady Meredith. What they cared about was the effect on the team.

"I'd say it would have worse effect on the people who bet money with Ford," Rhodes said, looking straight at Tandy. "Especially if they thought they had something to lose if Ford's records were ever made public."

Tandy swallowed hard and spooned up some

beans. Ballinger stirred his spoon around in his bowl. Goober Vance perked up. He had been looking a little gloomy, but now he was looking positively cheerful.

"Are you implying that maybe somebody we know bet money with Ford?" he asked.

He was looking at Tandy when he said it, but Tandy was crumbling his cornbread into his beans and didn't look up.

"I'm not implying a thing," Rhodes said. "I don't have any ideas about that, and we'll probably never know. Ford's records are missing."

"Hack didn't tell me that."

"He might not have known. I don't think I mentioned it to him."

Vance took a little notebook and jotted a few lines in it with a retractable ballpoint pen. Then he set the notebook on the table and said, "Is there anything else I need to make my story more complete?"

"How about Brady Meredith's funeral?" Rhodes asked. "When's that going to be?"

"Today," Ballinger said. "Two o'clock."

Tandy looked at his watch. "Hour and a half from now."

Ballinger wiped his mouth with a paper napkin. "I'd better get on back to the funeral home. Have to make sure everything's organized just right."

"Is the funeral going to be there?" Rhodes asked.

"No. I don't have a room big enough for the crowd. It's going to be at the Methodist church."

Ballinger picked up his bowl and paper water cup

and left. When he had gone, Vance asked, "Will you be at the funeral, Sheriff?"

"Most likely."

"What about you, Ron?"

Tandy blinked rapidly. "I'll be there. Right now, I have to get back to the office. I have someone coming in to look at a house at one."

He got up and carried his paper bowl to the trash can and dumped it in.

"I wonder why he got so upset when you mentioned about people betting with Hayes Ford," Vance said.

Rhodes shook his head. "I have no idea."

"I think you do," Vance said, "but I won't push it."

"Just as well that you don't," Rhodes told him.

The sheriff looked around the Dairy Queen. No one was paying any attention to him and Goober Vance. Everyone seemed to have lost interest in Rhodes when he sat down, and there was so much chatter that Rhodes didn't think there was much chance of anyone overhearing his conversation with Vance.

So he said, "What about you, Goober? Did you ever put down a bet with Hayes Ford?"

Vance pretended shock. "Are you kidding? I write about the games for the paper, but I don't bet on them."

Rhodes took a bite of his cornbread. There was just enough jalapeño to flavor it and give it a little bite.

"And you don't know anyone who does?" he asked Vance.

Vance picked his notebook up off the table, folded it, and put it back in his pocket.

"I'm not sure I understand what you're getting at, Sheriff," he said.

"Let me start over then," Rhodes said. "I've been looking into all those things you told me about on Saturday at the newspaper. Most of them were either exaggerated or led me in the wrong direction. I wonder why."

Vance had eaten all his beans, and there was nothing left in his bowl but the pot liquor. He sopped up some of it with part of a slice of cornbread and ate it.

"I still don't know what you're getting at," he said when he was through chewing.

"I'm getting at the fact that you might have a good reason not to like Terry Deedham."

"Who told you that?" Vance asked, reaching in his pocket for a toothpick.

"You reporters," Rhodes said, shaking his head. "Always asking questions when you should be answering them."

The toothpick wobbled from one side of Vance's mouth to the other.

"Ask me one, then," he said.

"I don't think so. I think I'll just tell you something."

"Whatever," Vance said.

"All right. See what you think about this. You weren't really interested in helping me find out who killed Brady Meredith at all. You were jealous of him because Terry Deedham seemed to like him, and you didn't really much care what had happened to him. But at least you were different from everyone else I've talked to. You didn't care about the football team. You saw it as a chance to get back at Terry. That's why you told me about her and Meredith, and that's why you told me about the steroids. You over-estimated me, though. I went off in the wrong direction."

Vance took the toothpick out of his mouth and looked at it. It was thoroughly chewed, and he replaced it with a fresh one.

"Do you think I killed Meredith because I was jealous of him?" he asked. "Because if you do, you're crazy."

Rhodes wasn't sure how crazy that idea was, but he said, "Maybe you didn't kill Meredith, but I think you know more than you're telling me."

"About what?"

"About Hayes Ford and about who bet with him."

"What makes you think that?"

"I'm not sure. Call it a hunch. When I asked you about whether Brady had ever bet with Ford, you said no. I thought then that you were trying to give me the idea that if it were true, you'd know about it. Now I think you *did* know about it."

Vance chewed his toothpick for a while. Then he said, "Let's say that I'd heard something. Would it have made any difference if I'd told you?"

"Maybe not," Rhodes admitted. "I found out soon enough from his wife that he'd very likely placed a few bets. But I'm still not sure why you didn't tell me."

"Because no matter what you think, I do care about the team. Maybe I did want to get back at the Deedhams, but from what I'd heard, nobody on the team had actually taken any steroids. So that couldn't be used against anyone. I just wanted to throw a little scare into Bob Deedham."

Rhodes thought that if scaring Deedham had really been Vance's plan, it hadn't worked very well. Deedham had been inconvenienced, but he hadn't been scared.

"But if Meredith had been gambling," Vance continued, "that was a real problem. God knows what the UIL would do to the team if that got out, and I didn't want to be the one to let the cat out of the bag."

"You didn't," Rhodes said.

For that matter, no one had. As things stood, it was likely that no one would ever be able to prove that Meredith had bet with Ford, so the team's record was safe.

"Good," Vance said. "I may be petty, but I wouldn't want to hurt the team."

Vance, Rhodes decided, wasn't so different from everyone else in town after all.

THE CHURCH WAS FULL. Even the balcony, generally useful only at Christmas and Easter, was at capacity. Rhodes wondered how many people would be at the funeral of Hayes Ford. He didn't think Clyde Ballinger would have trouble finding a room large enough to hold them.

The front pews of the church were filled on one side by the members of Brady Meredith's family. On the opposite side the members of the Clearview Catamounts sat in front, most of them looking very uncomfortable in their dark suits, white shirts, and ties. The coaches, including Bob Deedham, sat with the team, and they didn't look much more comfortable than their players.

Rhodes, sitting at the rear of the church, listened while the organist played the familiar gospel hymns about gathering at the river, marching to Zion, standing on the promises, resting on the everlasting arms, and dwelling in Beulah Land.

The body of Brady Meredith lay at the front of the church in the casket, which was surrounded by flowers and wreaths. The top half of the casket was open, but from where he sat Rhodes couldn't see the body. He didn't mind.

He listened while the minister told everyone what a wonderful man Meredith had been, and how there was nothing finer than someone who devoted his life to teaching young people the values of sportsmanship and fair play. He didn't mention gambling.

Marynell Jones, who sang at a great many Clearview funerals, did her rendition of "How Great Thou Art."

Jerry Tabor, wearing his old letter jacket, which Rhodes wasn't sure was entirely appropriate to the occasion, delivered a brief eulogy in which he repeated most of the ideas the minister had already

expressed, which were pretty much the same sentiments Jerry had talked about to the football team in
the previous afternoon.

But then Jerry went further. He exhorted the Catamounts to let Meredith's life be an example to them.
He told them that they had to put the troubles of the
present aside and think of the future. They had to
remember that from somewhere "up there" Meredith would be watching them from a seat on "that
big fifty-yard line in the sky," a phrase that was wor-
thy of Goober Vance.

Practically everyone in the church was crying by
the time Tabor finished. Even Tabor was having dif-
ficulty choking back the tears.

After that, everything was anticlimactic. The casket was closed and rolled out of the church. The pall
bearers, including the coaches, lifted it into the back
of the hearse, which sat with its engine idling while
everyone told Nancy Meredith how sorry they were
for her loss.

Rhodes joined Buddy Reynolds to help direct the
traffic for the procession that wound its way to the
cemetery, where the minister read from scripture and
committed Meredith's body to the grave.

Buddy and Rhodes were standing a short distance
away from the grave site, watching. When the brief
service was over, Buddy said, "You got any ideas
about who did it, Sheriff?"

"Too many," Rhodes said, and they watched the
mourners get in their cars and drive away.

TWENTY

RHODES NEEDED TIME to think things over, but he didn't get it. Almost as soon as he got back to the jail, Hack took a call from the hospital.

Rapper and Nellie had left.

"Left?" Rhodes said, taking the telephone from Hack. "They just *left?*"

"You didn't leave any guards on their rooms," the hospital administrator said. "I just found out about it, myself."

Rhodes didn't bother to explain that he didn't have any deputies to spare for guard duty.

"What happened?" he asked.

"I don't really know. When the nurse went to check on them a few minutes ago, they were just gone."

Rhodes had a sudden mental picture of the two bikers fleeing down the highway, straddling their bikes in their hospital gowns, the tails flapping in the breeze.

But he knew that couldn't happen. The bikes had been impounded.

"You'd better have everyone on the staff check the parking lot," he told the administrator. "There might be a car missing."

"Ohmigod."

The phone clattered in Rhodes's ear, and then he heard the busy signal.

"Call Buddy and have him get over there," Rhodes told Hack. "Tell him to check with the administrator. If there's a car missing, get out a bulletin on it."

Even as he said it, he knew it was too late. If they'd stolen a car, Rapper and Nellie would abandon it at the first opportunity and steal another one.

When Hack finished his call to Buddy, he said, "I guess they won't be comin' back here for sure after this."

"Why not?" Rhodes asked. "What do they have to be afraid of?"

"Car theft, for one thing."

"Even if there's a car missing, how are we going to prove they stole it? Someone will have to see them in it, or we'll have to catch them in it. Otherwise they'll just wipe the prints and laugh at us if we accuse them."

"It ain't right," Hack said.

"It's just a game to people like Rapper," Rhodes told him.

"Well, we still got him on all those charges you wrote up on him this mornin'. If he ever comes back, we can stick him for those."

"It's a thought," Rhodes said.

"Besides, maybe he's the one killed Brady Meredith. That'd put him away for a while."

"Not long enough. And I don't think he did it, anyway."

"Why not?"

Rhodes explained about Rapper's curious lack of enthusiasm for leaving the county when he had the chance.

Hack thought it over. "You may be right. A guy like Rapper, you give him a chance to leave, he'd take off like a scalded dog if he thought there was a chance of goin' down for murder."

"He wanted to wait until he got his money from Bob Deedham," Rhodes said. "I don't think he knew about the murder."

"Yeah. Even Rapper ain't crazy enough to risk a murder charge for a few hundred dollars."

"Maybe not. But Nellie didn't mind taking a few shots at me this morning."

"They was just mad," Hack said. "I expect they got to thinkin' about the consequences, and that's why they left the hospital. They thought about what could happen to 'em when you added attempted murder to the charges you already had against 'em, and they decided it was time to take off. Anyway, from what you said about 'em, they must've walked out of there. They sure couldn't run."

There was some comfort in that thought, but not much. It was just another thing that Rhodes didn't have time to worry about, however. He had to sort through his suspects and try to find out who had murdered Meredith and Ford before anyone else got killed.

THERE WERE PLENTY of people in the courthouse on a Monday. Some were there to get their license-plate renewal stickers, some were there to serve on juries, some were there to file deeds, some were there to pay taxes, and some were there just to loaf around and see what gossip they could pick up.

Everyone Rhodes passed on the way to his office stopped him to ask about his progress on the murders. It was worse than the Dairy Queen.

There was one bit of good news, and that came from Gerald Bonny. The lawyer was wearing a dark suit and carrying a soft leather briefcase. He was there on behalf of a client who was accused of violating the terms of his probation, but Bonny had time to pull Rhodes aside and tell him that the Garton coaches had decided not to pursue the idea of taking their case against the referees to court.

"They knew they didn't have a chance," he said. "I think they just wanted to get everyone all stirred up about it. I don't think they ever intended to go through with it."

Rhodes told him he was relieved to hear it.

"Everyone is. But what about those murders? Have you arrested anybody yet?"

Rhodes admitted that he hadn't.

"Damn. It's going to tear this town apart if we don't win this week. Getting into the play-offs is the biggest thing to happen here since...well, I can't think of anything this big except the oil boom, and I'm not old enough to remember that. People are going to spend more money in the stores, they're going to feel closer as a community, they're going to get behind the schools...it would be great if it weren't for those two murders."

Rhodes nodded. He didn't know what else to do.

Then he got a Dr. Pepper from the machine in the hall and went on to the office, where he closed and locked the door behind him. He didn't turn on the light because he didn't want anyone to know he was there. He sat at his desk and drank the Dr. Pepper and thought about all the people who might have a motive for killing Brady Meredith.

Would Jasper Knowles have killed his assistant coach because Meredith threw a punch at him?

Rhodes didn't think so. A real hothead might do something like that, but Knowles seemed like the kind of man who didn't let stress and pressure affect him.

Bob Deedham? He didn't show any signs of jealousy at all. Football would always be first in his affections, with his wife a very distant second. He might not have liked Meredith, but he had no real reason to kill him.

Goober Vance? As far as Rhodes could tell, he had practically no connection with Meredith at all outside of his duties as a reporter.

Rhodes had already virtually eliminated Rapper and Nellie. They were interested in selling drugs to Deedham, and they might have killed someone who got in their way, but there was no evidence that Meredith had interfered at all except to sermonize to the football team about the evils of drugs.

Which brought Rhodes back to Deedham. Would he have killed Meredith because of what Meredith might have said or done had he known that Deedham was considering feeding steroids to the Catamounts?

Not very likely. There might have been a scene, maybe even a fist fight, but not murder.

Terry Deedham? She didn't have a motive.

Nancy Meredith? Same answer.

Rhodes drained the Dr. Pepper bottle and set it on the desk. He knew he was overlooking something, but he couldn't quite put his finger on it.

Was he looking for the wrong things? Could it be that Hayes Ford had killed Meredith and then been murdered himself?

That made at least a little bit of sense. If Ford had lost a lot of money on the Garton game, he might have blamed Meredith. And he might have been angry enough to kill him. But if that was the way it had happened, who had killed Ford?

Rhodes shifted his mental gears. Who had the most to lose if it came out that Meredith had been gambling and shaving points?

The answer to that one was easy: The Clearview Catamounts. Everyone in town had been telling that to Rhodes for the last couple of days.

Rhodes considered the idea. Had he made a mistake by not investigating the members of the football team more closely?

The entire case, from beginning to end, had been about winning football games. The whole town seemed convinced of the importance of victory in the play-offs; that was what mattered, not the fact that two people had died.

Bob Deedham had believed, at least until recently, that winning was all that mattered, even if you had to cheat by using drugs to do it.

Brady Meredith had believed, or so Rhodes thought, that as long as you won, it didn't matter if you shaved a few points off the final score.

Even Judge Parry had come by Rhodes's house to talk to him about how important it was for the town to have a winning team.

So how did the team feel? Would one of the Catamount players have killed Meredith if the coach's gambling had been a threat to the team?

It was possible, but Rhodes didn't believe it.

And if that wasn't possible, who was left?

Nobody. Nobody else cared that much about winning.

Except maybe the members of the Catamount Club.

And then the whole picture shifted in Rhodes's head and he thought he had the answer.

THE DEL-RAY CHEVROLET Company was located a few blocks from the courthouse and just a block away from what was left of the Clearview business district. The big Wal-Mart at the edge of town had drawn most of the potential customers away from the downtown, and there were as many vacant buildings as there were occupied ones.

Del-Ray wasn't a modern dealership. It had been in the same building for as long as Rhodes could remember. There was room for one car in the showroom; all the other new models were parked on vacant lots beside the building and across the street.

The used-car lot was a block farther along. It looked a little cheap and gaudy, with ropes of red and yellow plastic flags that snapped in the late afternoon breeze.

The office was a little prefab metal building in the middle of the lot. To get to it, Rhodes had to walk by cars with ALL POWER! and FULLY LOADED! and MAKE US AN OFFER! whitewashed on the windshields.

He'd gotten about halfway to the office when Jerry Tabor, still wearing his letter jacket, came out to meet him.

"Looking for a good used car, Sheriff?" he said. "I can put you in one for just a little bit down and only a few dollars a month. Probably for less than your phone bill if you use long distance much."

"I'm not really in the market for a car," Rhodes said. "I just wanted to talk to you."

"We could go in the office," Tabor said.

Rhodes asked if the manager was there.

"Harry always leaves a little early," Tabor said. "I stick around in case a customer comes in."

He looked around hopefully, as if thinking a hot prospect might arrive at any minute, but there was no one in sight.

"This won't take long," Rhodes said.

"Sure. Great. Let's go."

Tabor led Rhodes to the office, which was divided into two tiny compartments by a thin partition. The whole thing smelled strongly of smoke. There was an overflowing ashtray on Tabor's desk.

"Have a seat, Sheriff," Tabor said, going behind his desk and sitting down.

Rhodes sat in the wooden chair beside the desk. He looked in the ashtray. There were quite a few Marlboro butts, and, in fact, there was a red and white pack of Marlboros lying in the middle of the desk.

"You smoke?" Rhodes asked.

Tabor laughed weakly. "Only when I'm nervous. About a sale or something."

"Then you won't need to now," Rhodes said.

"I guess not," Tabor said, but he didn't sound convinced. "What did you want to talk about."

"About you killing Brady Meredith."

Tabor sat very still for almost a minute. Then he reached for the Marlboro pack, saying, "Maybe I do need a cigarette after all."

TWENTY-ONE

RHODES DIDN'T OBJECT, and Tabor lit up. After he exhaled, he picked up the ashtray and dumped its contents into a wastebasket under his desk. His hand was a little shaky, and the ashtray clinked against the side of the wastebasket.

"You must have me confused with somebody else," he said, replacing the ashtray on the desk. "I didn't kill anybody."

"I think you did," Rhodes said. "I just wish I'd thought about it sooner."

Tabor tapped his Marlboro on the edge of the ashtray. His hand trembled.

"Why would I kill anyone?" he asked.

"How many cars have you sold in the last month or so?" Rhodes asked. "A lot more than usual?"

"I guess so, but what does selling cars have to do with anything?"

"A lot, if you look at it in the right way. For years no one has paid much attention to you, and I know for a fact that you haven't been setting the woods on fire as a car salesman since you got on here at Del-Ray. But now you're a local celebrity. Everyone knows who you are. You get invited to speak to the football team and at the pep rallies at the high school. You were even asked to speak at Meredith's funeral. I think you enjoy the attention, and the longer the

team keeps on winning and stays in
the state title, the more attention you
come by to talk to you here at the lot. So
even buy cars.''

Tabor crushed out his cigarette and look
butt. Rhodes waited for a few seconds, but
didn't say anything.

Rhodes said, ''This afternoon I remembered
you didn't show up for the Catamount Club on S
urday, and that reminded me of something else
When Meredith left the field on Friday night, you
were following him. I wonder if he happened to run
into Hayes Ford in the parking lot? He'd gotten
pretty careless about meeting Ford, and you might
have seen him. You might even have overheard them
talking. And you would have known what a conversation between a coach and a known gambler would
mean if the wrong people found out about it.''

''I never saw them,'' Tabor said. ''It never happened.''

''Something like it did,'' Rhodes said. ''And then
you went home for your pistol. I wouldn't be surprised if you didn't still have it at home. A profes-
sional would have gotten rid of it, but you wouldn't.
You wouldn't think like that.''

''I don't have a pistol,'' Tabor said, his voice so
low that Rhodes hardly heard him.

''Sure you do. And we'll find it. Anyway, I think
you followed him when he left the field house and
used the pistol to persuade him to drive down to the
woods below the stadium. Then you had a little talk
and found out for sure that Meredith had been betting

ng points, too, but maybe

' Tabor said, but he had

viction.

'' Rhodes said. ''You

, because he probably

.ecords, by the way?''

or said, looking at the ash-

I figured. You did pretty well, but
a few mistakes. You wiped the car, but
got the ashtray. There's DNA in saliva, Jerry,
and there'll be saliva on the cigarette butt you left
there. We can put you in the car.''

''I didn't mean to kill him,'' Tabor said.

''I think you did,'' Rhodes said. ''On Saturday,
you told the team that nothing could stop them. What
could have stopped them before? Someone finding
out about Brady's gambling?''

''He shouldn't have gambled. It was stupid. He
was going to ruin everything.''

''Not if no one found out.''

''I couldn't take that chance. There he was, right
there in the parking lot, and Hayes Ford was yelling
at him. I thought everybody in town would hear
them. I went over and told them to shut up. It scared
Brady, but Ford was mad and tried to keep talking.
I got Brady away from him.''

''And told him you'd meet him after the game?''

''We needed to talk. But he told me to get away
from him, that it wasn't any of my business.''

''So you got the pistol.''

"Yes. But it was just for persuasion. I wasn't going to kill him."

"But you did," Rhodes said.

Tabor picked up the Marlboro pack and stared at it as he turned it in his hands.

"He tried to take the pistol away from me," he said finally. "It went off by accident."

"It wasn't an accident that you killed Ford."

"No. I had to do it. He called me, Saturday afternoon after I talked to the team. He said he knew I'd killed Brady and that he was going to tell you unless I paid him off. He wanted a thousand dollars. I couldn't afford to pay him a hundred dollars, much less a thousand. And he said he was going to tell about Brady's gambling, too. He had the records to back it up. I had to do something."

"How did he know you killed Brady?"

"He was just guessing. Maybe I said some things in the parking lot, but he didn't know for sure. He couldn't have."

In a way, Rhodes felt sorry for Tabor. Winning had meant more to him than to anyone. For years he hadn't had a life, and this year the Catamounts had given one back to him. To keep it, he'd killed two men.

"I guess we'd better go on over to the jail, Jerry," Rhodes said.

Tabor looked at his watch. "I don't get off for another half-hour yet."

Rhodes stood up. "I'll talk to Harry for you."

"I guess it's all right, then. Can I have a minute to lock up the office?"

"Take your time," Rhodes said.

No one was happy with the way things turned out, Jack Parry least of all.

"I can't believe this," he said when he caught up with Rhodes at the jail. "Jerry Tabor was a local hero. Why couldn't you have arrested some bum who was just passing through town?"

"Because it wasn't some bum who killed Meredith and Ford," Rhodes told him.

"I know that. You know what I mean."

Rhodes agreed that he did.

"There's some good news, though," Parry said.

"What?" Rhodes asked.

"As far as anyone can find out, there's no way to prove that Meredith was actually betting on the games. Ford's records are gone, and Ford sure can't testify."

"What about Tabor?"

"The word is that he's going to try to avoid a trial. But even if he's tried and it comes out that his motive was to cover up for Brady's gambling, it won't matter. There's still no proof. Is there?"

Rhodes admitted that there wasn't. "But the Garton coaches might decide to file a complaint with the UIL," he said. "They wouldn't have any trouble getting most of the other coaches in the district to go along with them."

"They might try it, but it wouldn't do them any good. No proof."

Rhodes thought Parry was probably right. It was too bad, but Tabor, while he wasn't going to get away with murder, was going to succeed in keeping the Catamounts in the play-offs.

"God knows how the team is going to deal with this," Parry said. "With Jerry in jail and accused of murder, things are worst than before."

"The team will probably surprise you," Rhodes said. "I think they can handle it."

Parry sighed. "I hope so. Are you going to be at the game?"

Rhodes said that he hadn't thought about it. The game would be played out of town, at a neutral site.

"You should be there. God, I hope we win. It'll mean a lot to Clearview. Maybe I'll see you in the stands."

"Maybe," Rhodes said. But he didn't think so.

MURDER FLIES LEFT SEAT

JACKIE LEWIN

A GRACE BECKMANN MYSTERY

Grace Beckmann would prefer solid ground any day to the glory, freedom…and sheer terror of riding shotgun in her husband's beloved Piper Turbo Arrow. So when the couple arrive at the airport to find their plane stolen, Grace breathes a silent prayer of thanks. Unfortunately, the small aircraft is found crashed in the Rockies, with the body of a good friend inside, a victim of sabotage.

Was is supposed to be them? Was the crash carefully planned to ground the Beckmanns…permanently?

Available August 2000 at your favorite retail outlet.

Take 2 books and a surprise gift FREE!

SPECIAL LIMITED-TIME OFFER

Mail to: **The Mystery Library™**
3010 Walden Ave.
P.O. Box 1867
Buffalo, N.Y. 14240-1867

YES! Please send me **2 free books** from the Mystery Library™ and my free surprise gift. Then send me 3 mystery books, first time in paperback, every month. Bill me at the bargain price of $4.44 per book plus 25¢ delivery and applicable sales tax, if any*. There is no minimum number of books I must purchase. I can always return a shipment at your expense and cancel my subscription. Even if I never buy another book from the Mystery Library™, **the 2 free books and surprise gift are mine to keep forever.**

415 WEN C23C

Name	(PLEASE PRINT)	
Address		Apt. No.
City	State	Zip

AILEEN SCHUMACHER

A TORY TRAVERS/ DAVID ALVAREZ MYSTERY

AFFIRMATIVE REACTION

Tory Travers planned to spend her afternoon crawling through a storm drain in an unfinished housing development project. She was looking for a leak. Instead she found a corpse.

When Detective David Alvarez arrives on the scene, romantic and political tensions heat up. The victim is Pamela Case, a county commissioner who has a tainted political history with the abandoned housing complex. Her murder exposes a life—and death—entangled in graft, corruption, suicide and blackmail.

Available July 2000 at your favorite retail outlet.

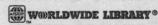